Dear Willi

Amazing ma

Lots of love,

William x

Life Run

MM Williams

TILDEN PUBLISHING

For Piers, Hugh,
Amy and Will

We hope you enjoy this book.

As an independent publisher, word of mouth is so important. If you do, please spread the word.

@tildenpublishing

Chapter 1

What was meaningful and what held little value all changed places in that instant, but Lisa would not realise this for some time. She tried to think but she couldn't. Cracks in the universe began to appear, a rug pulled from under her feet revealed nothing below.

She didn't move, but glanced at the empty seat next to her, then back to Sara and the grave face she was wearing. It was supposed to be a one-in-a-million check-up, and in her book, one in a million could mean 'discountable' or 'impossible', but specifically, 'would never happen to me'. *We found something.*

She half expected Sara to smile and say something like, 'We're being extra cautious. It pays to be cautious with your health.' At this point, she heard her own voice interacting with her friend, reacting to the information as if two other people were having this conversation.

Sara said, 'There's plenty more we need to talk through, but there's also material on the NHS website that will be helpful.' Something gave Lisa away – perhaps the lack of a discernible reaction – so that Sara gently reached across the desk and placed her hand on hers. 'We'll get through this, don't you worry. The next step is to arrange another appointment with Dr Stevens when he's back.'

Rain tapped outside and Lisa began to stir. Firstly, it shouldn't have been Sara giving her this news. Dr Stevens, the neurologist, should have called but he had been on holiday. Secondly, there was the school run. She stood up, her hand sliding away from Sara's. 'Sorry, Sara. The children need to get to school.' This mundane piece of her day, this insignificant, irritating fact of life, was now a life raft of normality from the world of a moment ago, before she had stepped into Sara's office.

'Lisa? Please sit, it's okay. We need more time to discuss this.' Sara grabbed some leaflets on her desk and held them out as a last gasp. Lisa took them in a careful swoop so as not to snatch, folding them into her coat pocket. 'I'm sorry,' she said. 'I don't have time. I was supposed to be picking up results. The children are waiting in the car.' She went for the door.

'Lisa?'

'No, I can't. Not now.'

'Please come back,' said Sara, but her voice was already in another room as Lisa closed the door to the surgery and found herself looking down at faces looking back at her – other patients sitting on plastic chairs down one side of the corridor, waiting for appointments of their own. Conscious of them, she walked past following signs to the lift.

She pressed the button but after a few moments' wait she took the stairs which seemed to narrow at each flight until it was just her, the banister and the height she could fall from, all spiralling down.

In the reception area a small crowd sat or stood while their patience ran dry: knees shaking, fingers tapping and voices rising. The fissure between the world outside, where people went about their lives, and the world inside, where people became patients. She kept her head down, skirting round to the main entrance.

She pulled her collar up and stepped out into the downpour but approaching her car, Sara's words caught up with her, the phrase repeating itself over and over again: *We found something.*

She stood still as the world moved on, blurred, indifferent and yet watchful. She counted out the steps to the car, saying the numbers in her head, unaware she was muttering them too. She opened the door and got into the driver's seat. Done it. She grabbed the steering wheel and held it tight, arms stiff and knuckles white, as if driving too fast. In fact, she was still parked outside a hospital, holding on for dear life.

From the back of the car she heard faint tapping on electronic devices. She looked in the rear-view mirror and there they were, just as she'd left them: Max using every millisecond to game while Mummy quickly picked up test results; and Alice texting who-knows-who, intensely. She felt Max's feet gently kicking the back of her seat, which he often did without noticing.

'Darling, can you not kick my chair, please.'

'Sorry, Mummy,' he said.

And with that word 'Mummy', her circumstances began to take root. Just as she was getting ready to carry on, back to her life of school runs and commutes, she felt tears in her eyes and a lump in her throat because her son had just said 'Mummy' and the horizon that had always been so far away was now so close it blocked out life from view. No sports days, holidays, promotions or graduations. No nothing but Dr Stevens' diagnosis, delivered by Sara.

She had to get on with the day. She'd text Sara soon. It was probably nothing, this whole thing. She pushed everything to the back of her mind because she had the school run to do. In that moment, that's all there was to do. Still, the children needed to go to school.

'Mummy, you're soaking!' said Max, who had put down his Nintendo and unclicked his seatbelt, stooping under the car roof, putting his arms around her neck, then recoiling from his damp chauffeur.

'What's this?' said Alice. Lisa turned to see her pointing at her brother's shirt, a finger right on his belly button. He looked down and as he did, Alice's finger rose up and tapped his nose. 'Every time,' she said.

'No!' Max smiled and sat back down in his seat behind Lisa.

For a moment, Lisa forgot where she'd just come from and smiled at her two children. 'There she is! Who says my daughter's always glued to her phone.'

But she was met with hard, territorial eyes that said that her daughter's joke was to remain on this piece of land where she – the mother – was not welcome to walk.

'Actually, I was texting Aunt Chloe. Remember her?' said Alice. Lisa turned back and started going through her bag. 'And are you driving us to school, Lisa, or should we walk?' Her daughter let out a sigh full of impatience, reminding her that this child was lost to adolescence. She looked up into the rear-view mirror, Alice glaring back at her for perhaps as long as she dared, then out of the window and finally back to her phone.

Getting back into mother mode, after shell-shocked mode, was much easier for speaking to and dealing with her children. 'Okay, Alice, enough of that,' said Lisa, now in defensive mode, which was actually mother mode in disguise – a constant array of emotions and boundaries set so that she could 'get on with it'. Get on with the five thousand things that needed to happen in a family of four. Here, Lisa could deal with people, such as her daughter, who liked to take out a yardstick when any lightness of air dared to bring them closer.

And like that, life continued as Lisa pressed the button to start the car and put the heating fans on to defog the window and dry her clothes. The handbrake came off and they resumed the school run.

The engine hummed and the car's suspension bumped along and in the rear-view mirror Lisa kept glancing at Alice. She was proud of her daughter who had both eyes firmly set out of the window, towards a horizon of her own, all too keen to break out of the family. *Fair enough*, Lisa thought, *because family life can be so small*. She just wished her daughter could spare a thought for her mother, now and again.

At the gates of her school, Alice ruffled her brother's hair and turned to her mother: 'I hope the doctor's appointment went okay.'

'All good,' said Lisa. Her daughter picked up her rucksack and got out the car. 'Next time you text her, send Aunt Chloe my love, please,' she added.

With another flash of the eyes, Alice said, 'You are more than capable of communicating with your own sister.' She swung the car door shut and like that, she was off to school.

Lisa watched her walk up to a group of girls in her year huddling together, laughing and talking loudly. Her daughter looked back and Lisa waved but Alice shrugged and walked off with her friends.

She looked at her son's reflection in the rear-view mirror: 'right, you next.' He met her gaze and for a moment, that's all there was, just the two of them in the whole world.

*

Once they'd dropped off his sister, Max went back to his game, playing as silently as he could because he knew one word from his mother and he'd have to give it back. Each moment was vital; he'd only been allowed to bring it on the school run today because she was seeing the doctor. It was a treat.

Between side-quests, losing lives and killing monsters, he kept glancing out of the window to see where they had got to and how long he had left to play. He decided to stop before his mother noticed – that way he could play at breaktime in the toilet with Mo, or in the classroom when his classmates were in the playground. It ran the risk of being confiscated and then he'd not get it back until the end of term. He saved his game and slid the console into his rucksack. Something was unusual about this morning but he couldn't quite put his finger on it.

The journey continued quietly and he looked to the window, following the raindrops on the surface. The rain had eased off and he wanted to see which droplets would make their way down the glass. Some were blown together as the car moved along, becoming one larger droplet that fell satisfyingly quickly. They reminded him of Alice's tears trickling down her cheek last night, as he watched her through a crack in the door.

It occurred to him that his mother had said nothing since they'd dropped off Alice and he craned forward to see her face. She didn't even react to him leaning forward; usually, she'd ask him to sit back down. 'Hi, Mummy,' he said.

'Hello, darling.'

She didn't say anything else, which was even stranger. She should be asking him questions about school lunches, lessons and games kit. At the traffic lights he said, 'Can I come and sit up front with you?'

'Darling, I don't think there's time.'

'I'll be really quick.' He'd already unbuckled his seat belt, the car still stopped at the lights.

'Okay, then. Be quick!'

He stepped over the armrest between the front seats, sat down in the passenger seat next to his mum and, reaching up, drew down the seatbelt, clicking it in just in time, before the car moved off again. Now with access to the controls, he pressed the heated seat button for both seats. 'I put the warmer on,' he said.

'Thank you.'

Up front, the windows were still fogged up at the bottom and he started drawing smiley faces with his finger, but when he ran out of space, the silence urged him on. 'Are you okay, Mum?'

'Yes, I'm fine,' she said, concentrating on the road. 'Is everything okay with you?' she asked.

Max thought about school. He didn't want to go in. He wondered if it was worth a try saying he felt sick. He did feel sick, the thought of school made him feel sick, but he didn't want to tell his mother that so he said, 'I'm fine too.'

For the rest of the journey, he wondered what his sister had been crying about. He found his older sister so intriguingly mysterious, he could only guess at her world. Her life stretched more outside than his, beyond school, home and playdates. He didn't understand what or why she did what she did and said what she said.

At his school gate, his mother parked the car on the other side of the road and told him to wait as she stepped out on her side. Standing on the pavement, she reached back and took his rucksack out. There was a moment when he thought she was taking his game console back, but she handed the bag to him, took his hand and they crossed the road together.

*

Max had asked many times that she not hug him at the school gate, but this time he let her. She wondered if he sensed that, today of all days, she needed a hug, even if he did go stiff in her arms. 'Mum,' he said, 'it's raining.'

She let go and watched him run through to the courtyard, up the stairs and out of sight. It was hardly raining, she complained, and it was looking like the day might clear up.

Back in the empty car she sat for a moment with the engine off. Her coat was soaked through and pressed against her skin. She wanted to go home, have a hot shower and change into dry clothes. To start the day again, as if the first attempt could be discounted, along with everything that had happened so far.

There were a couple of meetings meetings at the office, client pitches for new business. They were her bread and butter, she wouldn't need to prepare for them and there was nothing for the first half of the morning. She emailed a junior on her team that she'd be in later than expected, pushed the button for the engine and began the drive home.

She drove without the radio on, not really thinking, letting muscle memory do the driving. On the High Street, not far from home, a parking space offered itself outside a café she'd normally only go to on a rare, spare Saturday morning. She pulled over and walked in.

The café was busy with early morning workers. Running parallel to the queue was an array of sandwiches, croissants and juice bottles. When it was her turn she ordered a coffee and stood at the other end of the bar. As she waited her hands went into her coat pockets and feeling something she didn't recognise, she pulled out the leaflets Sara had given her. A pang of adrenaline hit as she saw what they were. She went to the milk and sugar stand and held them over the bin, before folding them again and placing them into a side pocket in her handbag.

'Double espresso? Lisa.'

She found a table next to the window and stared out into space until her mind settled on Sara. She had been gentle with her in the appointment, but she'd ambushed her with the results. She took out her phone and texted:

> *I don't understand why you didn't explain the results last night when you texted. We could have covered that ground then, and I could have been more prepared this morning. For the record, I feel completely fine. Can we get a second opinion, please. When is Dr Stevens back from holiday?*

She felt she should be a little more humble for treating one of her oldest friends like a doctor. Lisa added to the message: *I appreciate you're worried. Give me a day to think through all of this, and I'll read your leaflets.*

Sara was being overly cautious, irritatingly so. She was like that: very staid and risk-averse – all doctors were. She reread the messages she'd just sent, then added: *lots of love, L.*

The second text message she sent was to her husband: *Got caught in a shower on the school run, need to go home and change.*

She placed the phone on the table. She breathed in deeply then out again strongly and one or two other customers looked at her and she gave a curt smile back. She was already tired and it wasn't yet eight thirty. Her phone vibrated, it was Laurence.

'Hi love, won't you be late for work?' he said. Lisa didn't like it when he called her 'love' but she ignored it.

'I'm soaked through, I'm not going to spend the rest of my day trying to dry myself out in the office for my meetings in the afternoon.'

'Oh, okay. I might miss you as I've stepped out for a coffee. How long will you be at home for?'

'So much for working from home! Just having a coffee myself but I'm driving back now. I'll probably be gone in thirty minutes. Maybe see you in a bit. Kiss.'

'See you if I see you,' he said back. Then after a pause, 'Was the doctor's appointment okay?'

'Absolutely fine. They said they could do more tests but there's not much point.'

'Great news. Right, see you tonight, if not in a bit.'

Driving along towards home, it felt like she had a passenger. She checked the mirror but couldn't see anyone else. Another child she'd forgotten to drop off? Did Max forget his packed lunch? Was there an early morning meeting in the office that had slipped her mind? She named it a phantom when she couldn't find it, then tried to ignore it and focus on the last few minutes' drive home. The rush-hour traffic was slowly subsiding and this made her feel late, even if it helped her along, as if everybody else was now ahead of her in the day.

The sun was bright and glaring now and she felt fine. She kept on trying to listen to her body to see if it could tell her anything. An itch by her ankle, a muscle overstretched somewhere but nothing in her head. She did feel fine. She pulled the sun visor down and the closer she got to home, the more acute she felt this new phantom, this passenger in the car.

She said out loud, 'Who's there?' as people sometimes did when they were alone. But the passenger in her car wasn't a person, it wasn't a task she'd forgotten to do or a diary appointment she'd missed.

It was the new secret she was already keeping from her husband – her diagnosis.

Chapter 2

Sometimes, when Lisa walked through the front door the hallway seemed perfectly tidy, and other times it looked like chaos, but always the hallway was actually the same: stuffed with old clutter. It was the logistics centre of their family of four. A complex queue, or backlog, of items that needed processing, either under or on top of the slim table next to the wall, by the coat stand. The small bag of dead batteries that needed to be specially dispensed at the supermarket bin; a muddy little pair of football boots stacked on top of someone else's office shoes; letters opened and unopened; coins. Then the items that ended up there because... well, where else? Pens, some working, some not; redundant keys in a bowl, kept in case they opened some forgotten door; rubber bands. The dog leads and poo bags.

Today, she dropped her keys on the side table and walked down the hall to the kitchen, opening the door to Sebastian who wagged his tail and jumped up, all four paws off the floor. She crouched down and calmed him and once he was settled, she slid to the floor, back resting against a cupboard, stroking the little dog. After a minute or so she put him back in his bed.

When she got out of the shower she saw a missed-call notification and a number of texts from Sara and swiped to remove them from her home screen. She got dressed slowly, chose smarter clothes than the ones she'd begun the day with, slipped on her backup pair of dry trainers with her heels in her bag.

Ready, she walked downstairs back into the kitchen and this time noticed breakfast still on the table. A splodge of jam here, crumbs everywhere else. On autopilot, she stacked the plates and put them in the sink.

'Laurence's problem,' she said, backing away from the dishes, palms out in surrender. She grabbed her handbag and closed the kitchen door to keep the dog inside.

On a whim, rather than head out the front door she took a right into the living room and stood there in the middle between the furniture and walls. There was a corner filled with Max's toys, grown dusty as the Nintendo swallowed his attention. She realised she hadn't taken it off him after the car journey, and there'd be a good chance it would be confiscated. He'd probably outgrown all the toys except the Lego, and even this he played with less and less. The redundant ones needed to be put in the hallway and donated to a charity shop. She fished out a stray Lego man and held it tightly in her hand.

The brand-new coat she'd bought Alice was on the back of the sofa and she placed it on a peg in the hall. It was funny – what other word was there for it? – how transient the gratitude of a teenager was.

She walked over to the bookshelves and read some titles out loud as her finger ran across the spines. Picking out one or two of her favourites, remembering not just the stories in them but where she was when she read them, where she'd been in life: relaxed mode, graduate mode, spare-time-to-read mode.

Most of the books were hers, some were Laurence's, but none of them were *their* books. It intrigued her that genres were too particular to ever be co-owned. Hers were contemporary, classic and literary; his were action, historical and science fiction. Tastes distinguished an individual and didn't blur into a marriage like furniture or kitchen utensils, or whatever else people brought to a new home when they moved in together. This begged the question, whether it was sensible to choose a partner with similar tastes in books or films. If that was true, then she hadn't been sensible.

We found something. The phrase Sara had used before the CT scan, was a 'check-up', which Lisa had interpreted as 'will not happen to you'. She tried not to think of the appointment. She put the Lego man into a sitting position with one hand in the air, as she liked to imagine Max, straining to answer a question in class, happy, learning and surrounded by friends. She left it on a shelf, angled so it could watch people come and go.

The room was still from echoes of activity: the flopping on the sofa, the chatting, the reading, the guests, the Christmas presents being opened by everyone in their pyjamas. Emptier because it was usually so full.

Lisa flopped on the sofa chair, and out of nowhere Sebastian jumped onto her lap. 'Jesus! How the heck did you get out of the kitchen, you little Houdini?' She kissed the dog on the head and stroked his fur backwards.

Sebastian gave her a blank look before making himself comfortable by circling twice and pawing at her thighs. Of all the dogs in the world, none were so pampered and yet appeared so homeless. Mad black-wire hair came out in all directions on a skinny little frame with a short nose.

Lisa paused for a moment as she watched the dog curl up to sleep on her lap and said, 'Sebastian, I've got a tumour.' The dog raised his head and gave another blank look which was always his answer to human dialogue. 'It's the size of a golf ball and it's in my brain,' she said, 'but I feel absolutely fine.'

On alert, Sebastian glared in the direction of the front door and she felt the vibrations of a growl through his tiny ribcage. 'Do I tell him?' she asked.

Keys clanked into the lock and the familiar sound of the bolt opening and the door's hinges creaking as Laurence opened the door. It was followed by a thud that shook the house.

'Hello,' he said. 'You okay?'

'I'm fine,' she said turning to him, 'I'm just taking a moment to... think.'

Laurence looked a little perplexed, then possibly, dismissive? 'Okay. I guess I'll clear up breakfast.'

Gradually, Lisa sat up and Sebastian sighed in protest. 'Go on, off you get.' The dog jumped down and made his way back to the kitchen.

'Bloody hell,' she said. She could hear her husband clanging dishes into the dishwasher above music from the radio. She visualised the commute and the meetings ahead, stacked up, one on top of the other, with colleagues crowded round, all looking up to her. 'Fucking hell.' It was the last thing on earth she wanted to be doing, but she didn't give herself a choice. She went to the front door, put on a dry overcoat and said loudly, 'Bye, Laurence. See you tonight.'

He didn't hear her from the kitchen so she just left. She had to get on with her day.

Chapter 3

Lisa hadn't been in her office for more than a moment when one of her staff knocked on her door, asking about the client pitches that afternoon. Clearly, there was some apprehension among her team. With one eye still scrolling through emails, she asked them to gather the team in a meeting room and come and get her when they were ready.

However, her attention had fallen on two emails that stood out in her inbox: an executive committee meeting was being called by Adam for tomorrow; and another, where Adam had copied in the entire executive committee, wishing her luck for a client meeting. It put her on edge, as the executive meeting implied that Adam – before just an irritant – now held sway over Jack. She couldn't see how the meeting was necessary; it made her suspicious.

She took the stairs one floor up to Jack's office. His assistant was at her desk, outside. 'Hi Pam, is Jack around?'

'Let me see if he's free.'

'Don't worry,' said Lisa, 'I'll knock.' Pam looked ruffled but didn't stop her from knocking on the door and walking in. She was, after all, Jack's right-hand woman.

'Lisa,' he said, 'come on in. I've got five minutes before a call.'

She didn't take a seat. 'I won't be long. What's the committee meeting about tomorrow?'

'I think it's a strategy and pipeline meeting – run-of-the-mill stuff.' He leaned back in his chair, ran his fingers through thin hair and rested his palms behind his head. Lisa folded her arms.

'Why are we letting one of our more junior executives call a meeting? Adam doesn't have that authority. Plus, we all have day jobs to do.'

He shrugged the muscles around his mouth. 'I appreciate your sentiment. I think he – and the others – want some transparency on revenue coming in.'

'If he wants transparency on revenue, he could start by sending invoices to his own clients.'

Jack laughed. 'Look, let's not make this too political. Why can't the other execs have a look at what your pipeline's bringing in?'

She cocked an eyebrow and said, 'Fine.' But beneath the meeting, she could see clearly a simple fact: Jack, as CEO, was being forced to call more committee meetings to keep other executives in line. His authority was ebbing.

'So, see you tomorrow,' he said.

'Sure,' she said, 'but Adam's email this morning, the one wishing me luck with everyone else on copy, was pretty snide.'

'Come on! It was inert at worst,' he said.

'Don't be naive. Adam saw an opportunity to belittle me, and took it.'

'I think you're being a tad sensitive.'

'Be careful, Jack. He will stab you in the back.' With that, she turned and left.

'Bye Lisa,' Pam said as she strode away but Lisa didn't acknowledge her. She was done with this place, livid. Everything in the office seemed to coalesce against her. She felt the same emotion she had done throughout her career, of being a women in an environment otherwise dominated by men – disparaged and actively denigrated.

'Lisa?' She looked up to see a member of her team standing outside her office. 'We're all gathered in meeting room B.'

'Okay. Let's go,' she said.

The room was crowded with her staff, some sitting at the table and others leaning against the wall. They were a mix of men and women, consultants and engineers who helped manufacturers across the world build things more cheaply.

'Let's hear them,' she said and her staff ran through the two pitches for that afternoon.

Lisa tried focusing on the slide decks and the accompanying spiel, but her mind kept slipping back to *We found something*. Sara should not have been the one to give her the results. As her close friend, it must have been weird. But on the other hand, she'd been wrong not to indicate the content of the results last night, when she'd arranged the appointment. She listened to her body again, there was no pain, she felt nothing in her head.

The mock pitches came to a close and Lisa encouraged her team to pick apart the presentations and make suggestions.

The room fell quiet as her staff deferred to her final say. 'The first pitch is fine. The second isn't ready. I can't be in the office today, so pitch one can go ahead without me, but pitch two needs to be postponed.'

'Lisa, do you think that's necessary?' asked a senior team member. 'If you're there, we'll be able to blag it.'

'I'm not around this afternoon, so let's push the meeting back, sort the pitch out and I'll make sure we're in to see the client before the end of the month. Thank you, everyone. Good work.'

One or two of the more senior staff stayed behind to try and change her mind, no one asked why she suddenly couldn't make it. Once they left, she opened her phone and texted the first client: *Hi Jane. Normally, I never miss a pitch. Some health issues have come up – you'll be in safe hands. Or would you prefer to postpone*?

A moment later, Jane's reply came through: *You've met everyone you need to. The pitch is a formality/makes no difference. Send your team over. Hope nothing serious. J x*

She called the second client on the speaker phone that sat in the middle of the meeting room table.

'Hi Lisa, how's things? We're seeing you in a bit, aren't we?'

'Hi Charlie. I'm sorry to do this, but we need to postpone our end. I can't be in the office for personal reasons and I want to be there myself when we meet your team.'

Her client gave a pause of irritation. 'That's a shame. We want to wrap up the tender process asap.'

'Can we rearrange before the end of the month?'

'Well, yes, I'm sure we can, but the sooner the better. If we find someone else in the meantime, we'll close the tender and go with them.'

They agreed to find another time through their assistants. It was eleven thirty and she had cleared her day. She returned to her office, conscious of one or two odd looks from people in her team. She rarely took an unscheduled day off and never cancelled client meetings. No one came up to her and questioned why she was unable to attend, which she assumed was owing to her slightly unapproachable manner.

She put on her overcoat, took off her heels and got back into her trainers, leaving the office for the day outside, which was damp but sunny.

She walked along the river adjacent to her offices which meandered towards a park. She took out her phone and read a message from Sara: *Please can you let me know you're ok. I'm worried.*

She was irritated by her concern, but Sara might text Laurence next if she didn't reply, so she stood to the side of the path and wrote: *Thanks, Sara. Give me a day, I'll be in touch.*

On a new line, sarcastically, she added: *I have your leaflets.*

But the last line reread as desperate, not sarcastic, and at that, she put her phone away and walked on.

The weather got worse again, cloudy with drizzle, which wasn't quite enough to abandon the walk, but enough for Lisa to skip the park bench she had planned to sit on in the sun. Instead, she walked on a little further, past a medieval church and onto a quiet street that had a café that was also a bookshop.

The first thing she did inside was check her emails. The rescheduled meeting had been put in her diary for the end of the following week. She sent an email to her team wishing them luck for the pitch later today.

She wanted to choose a book but hunger had caught up with her because she'd spent her breakfast feeding the children and getting Max's lunchbox fixed, while Laurence had showered late, eaten first and only then helped the kids get ready for school. She walked past the bookshop to the café at the back. It was empty but still cosy and had a menu written up on a chalkboard. She ordered soup and granola with fruit and yoghurt. At the counter, there was a sign with *Book of the Week* written on it, and a stack of copies of *Alice in Wonderland.* She picked one up and added it to her bill.

For the next couple of hours, Lisa read about cats that disappeared leaving their grin floating in the air, about babies that turned into piglets, and a Knave of Hearts put on trial by his king. Her parents had read it to her and she'd read it to her own children, Max only last year, and Alice years before that. She lost herself in those two worlds – the Wonderland of the book, and the bedtime world with her own children – and didn't think about pitches, or office politics and Adam. She didn't think about her husband who hardly spoke to her, but most of all, she didn't think about her appointment that morning.

After she finished the book she went to the shop at the front and picked up *Through the Looking Glass* and moved to a couch, but this time she didn't get far before she fell asleep. It took a moment to reorientate herself when she came round to her phone vibrating in her bag. She took it out – her sister was calling.

*

As a self-confessed people pleaser, Chloe couldn't help wanting not to irritate people but often – if not always – she didn't have a handle on quite how she affected those around her. Particularly, when it came to her sister, it was hard to have any interaction with her that didn't piss her off.

It hadn't always been that way but since their last argument, contact had only been through texts and calls. She wanted reconciliation, but felt only Lisa's exasperation when she called.

Today was no different. She needed to speak to Lisa about Alice and to do so would hurt her sister because Alice had decided to speak to her aunt and not her mother. But Chloe felt she had a duty to her sister. So, after she'd called their parents and practised some yoga and breathwork at home, she bit the bullet and called Lisa.

'Hi Lisa, sorry to call you at the office. I never know when I should call.'

'It's okay, I can talk.'

'You sound like you've just woken up.' Lisa said nothing back, so Chloe continued, 'I was calling about Alice, actually.'

'You seem to be texting a lot with her, which is nice.' Lisa's tone was tense.

'I want to say first, I feel I'm in a slightly uncomfortable position because I think she should have spoken to you before me.'

Her sister sighed loudly. 'It's okay, spit it out.'

'She called me up last night in tears. She wanted someone to talk to. It's tough, and I think she wanted it to be someone with a couple of degrees of separation – like her aunt and not her mother.'

'Chloe, imagine for a moment that I'm fine with whatever it is, and tell me.'

'You know Alice has been seeing someone from school? A boy in her year?'

'Yes,' said Lisa, but Chloe wasn't sure this was true.

'She got dumped by him, but apparently this boy is now seeing a friend of hers and there was some... *overlap*. I'm sure she'll speak to you when she's ready. It's just teenage growing pains.'

Chloe felt it was a good attempt at speaking to her sister, what with all the eggshells she had to tread on. Lisa's silence only served to make her more nervous, as if she might bring up their last argument.

'That's not teenage growing pains,' said Lisa after a moment, 'that's horrible. I'm glad she felt she could speak to you, if not me.'

'I'm sorry, I didn't want to call you up in the middle of the day and upset you with this, but like I said, I never know when to call.'

'Normally I'm busy nine to five. Is there anything else?'

'Have you spoken to Mum and Dad recently?'

'Not in the last week. Now's not a good time to catch up, Chloe.'

'It's never a good time. Can we see each other soon soon, please?'

'I'll call you later this week,' said Lisa. 'I promise.'

'Love you.'

'Yes, love you too.' Lisa hung up.

Chloe felt it had gone okay. She knew she'd have to call Lisa again, as she was the one propping up the relationship. It felt like her sister didn't want to prop anything up at the moment, apart from herself.

*

The problem with Chloe was that having her close meant having to put up with her comments, telling Lisa that she should work less or critique her marriage. Or she'd want to rake over some childhood memory, like when Lisa had pushed her into a pond. But never would she focus on her own life. Lisa suspected Chloe was relying on their parents for some of her income, for instance. But she was grateful that her little sister had been sheepish today; usually she was bombastic and it was scant recompense that Lisa's distance from Alice was replaced by closeness to her aunt.

A text vibrated onto her phone: *Don't tell Alice we've spoken, she wouldn't forgive me and I think it's good she's speaking to one of us. Lines of communication, and all that.*

Lisa didn't reply. She tried to go back to her book again but the conversation with her sister had jarred and her mind kept floating away while her eyes continued down the page, so that she had to reread the same paragraph over and over until she gave up. And then her mind was back to *We found something*, so she decided it was time to go back to the office.

She finished the day with one-on-one performance meetings with her team, asking about the support they were receiving from the managers between their positions and her own. She made sure to spend as much time with the junior team members as the senior ones, and in general, morale was high.

Lastly, she took the lift to the first floor, where the HR department was located. It wasn't a visit she relished, but this was the first time she'd made the journey for a matter unrelated to Adam.

She informed them she might need to take time out of the office, sporadically, over the next few weeks or months, for a health issue. They were insistent they know the details, but Lisa was hesitant because the situation with Adam didn't need any more intrigue or rumour.

Both parties compromised on an email from her doctor. 'We'll also need to inform your line manager,' they said. She smiled – she'd not had a manager in years. 'I suppose I report into Jack, the Chief Executive, or to the Board of Directors. But if at all possible, I'd rather they knew the absolute minimum. Ideally, nothing at all.'

'If you're going to be out of the office and business is going to be affected, we have to tell them that your absence has been explained to Human Resources.'

Again, they compromised – Jack should be informed there was an issue, but the nature of that issue would not be discussed. 'I doubt it will affect my work,' said Lisa, before leaving.

She got in the car. Laurence was picking up Max and cooking dinner. Alice was eating at a friend's. All she had to do was go home.

Chapter 4

Before she drove off, she sent a text to Sara: *Can you send an email to human resources at my office? The sensible first step, if I need time out of the office.*

It was just getting dark when she parked the car on the street outside her home. The lights were on. If she was lucky, Laurence would have dinner ready and Max would be doing his homework. Sara's reply was waiting for her on her phone:

Of course text me the email address. You should consider not working at all for the time being. Call me when you can.

Once again, Sara didn't get it. She didn't get it because she was a doctor and not a businesswoman, but if she'd stopped to consider the situation Lisa was in, she would have understood that other people's jobs depended on her, that her career meant a lot to her and that the house and home in front of Lisa now was mostly paid for via her job, Laurence's income covering far less than half their expenses.

She lifted her phone to her mouth and left a voice note: 'Hi Sara, thank you, I appreciate you doing that and I'll text the email address over soon. Under no circumstances can you tell HR what you told me. There's some serious office politics going on and I don't need the other executives knowing about this – and things like this have a habit of leaking out. I'm not taking a leave of absence at all but I am getting my ducks in a row. Speak soon.'

Couldn't Sara realise that Lisa was holding everything together? Jobs depended on her, the company needed her. And she wasn't about to go on a leave of absence for Adam to fill his boots. Sara was cautious by nature – overly so – but on the other hand, she was never dramatic, so there was that. But her friend's concern was irritating: she was always nice and kind and loyal and never anything else and that had a pull on Lisa that made her feel like the less decent of the two friends. She tried to remember the last time she and Sara had spent time together, without children or husbands.

But she didn't have time to deal with it now, so she slipped her phone into her bag and headed in and was hit by delicious smells of cooking, family life enveloping her. She walked into the kitchen, Laurence smiled at her and Max jumped up from the table that had his homework spread out and gave her a hug. She could tell her son was tired by how he leaned in to her.

'Dinner's almost ready,' said Laurence.

'Are you hungry?' she asked her son.

'I'm so hungry. I'm too tired to do any more homework.'

'You'll have to do it in the morning before breakfast,' said Laurence.

'Please?' Max begged.

'How many questions do you have left?' Lisa asked.

'Six.'

'Let's do them now. I'll help you,' she said. 'Can dinner wait five minutes?'

'Sure,' said Laurence and he turned off the hob, clanging lids onto pots. He went upstairs without saying anything else.

Max had eight, not six, questions left for his maths homework. She was surprised how hard they were for an eight-year-old, but he struggled through them with her help, her asking him questions that pointed him in the right direction, Max slowing down after each one as his energy and attention flagged. She answered the last one for him, telling him what to write down and why, then she turned the hob back on and shouted up the stairs for Laurence while Max put his homework into his school bag.

After dinner, Laurence took him up for a bath and a story while Lisa cleared the dishes. On the verge of tears that seemingly came from nowhere, she told herself how stupid it was to cry as she left the dishwasher unstacked and went into the living room. She sat down on the sofa, where Sebastian, following close behind, jumped on her lap.

When Alice was a child, she and Laurence would sometimes do story time together, one story each, the three of them as a family. They'd never done that with Max, maybe the novelty had worn off after eight years – the age gap between her children. Laurence used to read out the characters in funny voices for Alice. It was endearing and attractive, but he didn't do it for Max. After a while, he came down from story time and stood at the doorway to the living room. 'He fell asleep before I finished the story.'

She felt incredibly tired. Without looking at her, he flopped down on the sofa chair next to her, the springs crunching and cushions deflating. There they sat, in seemingly comfortable, exhausted silence. And as the silence spilled out, it hardened into something less comfortable so that Lisa's mind was not free to roam, but held there. Time slowed as the space between them became measurable in absent words, a language of its own.

She spied Laurence out of the corner of her eye. He was staring up at the ceiling, sitting next to her, not saying anything. The metaphor was there for the taking. She turned her head so that she joined him looking up at the ceiling.

The details of the doctor's appointment had melted away so that there was little tangible to remember. The appointment had become something more like an emotion, which pulled her down into loneliness and to pull herself up she knew she would have to talk about it.

But she didn't. She felt angry that the person with whom she should speak, who presented himself now, also placed himself far away from her. So she didn't say anything to Laurence. The silence showed how far their distance stretched, and she had no urge to break it because she wanted to witness how big it had become.

Maybe she didn't have to say anything. Maybe her face told the tale of her day, undeniable emotion etched on but for him to see it, he'd first have to look away from the ceiling, at her.

Uncertain, she countered herself: perhaps this moment was born out of fatigue and familiarity and she was misreading an intimacy they shared all along. A moment where they could open up by not saying anything at all.

'I'm tired,' she was saying.

'So am I,' he replied with his silence.

'This is life.'

'I know.'

'It's lucky we have each other.'

But then he wouldn't reply, his silence flipping to its real meaning: their distance and the nothing in between. She turned her head again to look at him. What were they saying to each other?

She recognised something very human in her that wanted to shatter the silence, to reach out over their distance and tell him she'd walked out of her appointment into the rain. Unable to tell him this, the urge became self-pity and tears welled up in her eyes while her husband continued to stare at the ceiling. She was tired. Tired like a mother; tired like someone diagnosed with a tumour; and tired like someone who didn't want to do another school run or go into the office ever again. She wanted to fold the distance, reach out and hold his hand but more than that, she wanted him to reach out and hold hers.

Gravity pulled back the tears. Sebastian nosed her hand and she petted his head. Laurence moved a muscle, then a leg, then his head turned and they made eye contact. Had it been a minute, maybe five, just sitting there? The two emotions she felt were hope and the humiliation of needing hope.

'I think I'm ready for bed. I'll do the rest of the washing-up and see you upstairs,' he said, acknowledging the flow of time and the passage of their marriage all at once. He got up, left the room and a moment later Lisa heard the clinks and clanks of the last of the washing-up.

What were they saying to each other? Nothing, no words at all. And it didn't really matter whose fault it was between them.

How had the ambitious, rather attractive architect she'd met become this shadow of himself? How could this romantic – who'd suggested she come off the pill before he proposed, such was his desire for her once upon a time – barely look at her? Whether their marriage was failing or simply evolving, she didn't know. But now she was suddenly angry. She stood up and the dog jumped down, surprised. She walked into the kitchen, stood next to him with her arms folded and said, 'Laurence?' She was so ready to scream, she could almost hear her scream before she opened her mouth.

He stopped washing the dishes and looked at her with tired eyes, suds scattered on his shirt. Anger slipped away, and in that moment she pitied him as much as she pitied herself.

'Yes?' he said apologetically.

She held back. She looked at him, his shirt sleeves pulled up, rubber gloves over his hands. She softened, 'It's nothing,' she said. 'I had a bad day at work.'

'Tell me about it in bed,' he said.

It was easier to get on with life this way, to preserve her home and her marriage. Climbing the stairs, she told herself that there was nothing in life she had not coped with before. The evolution of her marriage was just one more thing to deal with.

In bed together, she said, 'I remember so vividly, clutching a box of chocolates under one arm and holding a bunch of flowers in the other.'

'When was this?' Laurence asked.

'When I went on maternity leave for Max. I was saying goodbye to colleagues in the office, only a couple of weeks off my due date.'

'I remember. We'd just stopped house-hunting.'

'That's right. Anyway, out of the corner of my eye, I saw Jack and Adam together and it was the first time I'd seen them speak, standing with their backs to the wall, surveying the office floor. Jack had just been promoted to the executive committee, and I was head of our business line, reporting to him. We used to joke a lot back then that he'd hate the office politics whereas I could get on with the job and actually make money.'

'How long was your maternity leave? Only two months, right?'

'Three, I think. I remember, Jack said, "Adam here, will be caretaker for your clients while you're on leave."'

'Adam was given your clients?'

'It's normal for that to happen. Someone has to be point of contact for your clients while you're away. But it was that moment, right then,' Lisa lifted her head up from her pillow, propped up on her elbows, 'that I saw Adam flick a glance at Jack. And I remember thinking, *that's strange*. I didn't know that they knew each other well back then, but I didn't think about it too much – I had other things on my mind. But now I look back on it and realise that was the time Jack started hedging his bets with Adam.'

'And you think it's starting to backfire on Jack?'

'I've no doubt about it.' Lisa leaned back on the pillow.

Laurence said, 'I remember you told me what Adam said: "Enjoy maternity leave. I've got things covered here." And then he smiled at you in a way that really got under your skin and said, "Take your time."'

Chapter 5

Already yesterday seemed like a long time ago and the first thing Lisa remembered was the last thing that had happened the day before: Alice letting them know she was home as she wished them good night through their bedroom door.

Today, everyone was a little late, as if her own exhaustion had seeped into the family, so that when she came downstairs breakfast was going to be a rush. Laurence had his coffee and porridge in front of him and he'd made more for everyone else. Alice came down next and announced, 'I'm going to take the bus with Dad today.'

'Okay,' said Lisa. 'You'll be late if you don't get going. Here,' she sifted through her handbag and took out a five-pound note. 'Promise me you'll get breakfast at the school cafeteria.'

'I can give her money on the bus,' said Laurence.

'But I have it here,' said Lisa holding up the note a little higher. What point was he making?

'Thanks, Mum,' said Alice, pocketing the cash on offer. 'We should go, Dad.'

'Let me get my things.' And a moment later they were out the front door.

As Max hadn't appeared for breakfast she went looking and found him playing on his computer game. 'Not before school, darling. Yesterday was a treat.' Back in the kitchen she asked him, 'After your porridge, would you like scrambled eggs on toast? That's what I'm having.'

'Can I have fried eggs?'

'I don't have time to make both.'

'Please, Mummy.'

'I'm not your chef, Max. It's scrambled eggs or cereal.' He thought for a while before he agreed to scrambled. Lisa was impatient to get going as Max finished his food, but she didn't say anything while he ate, instead she packed the dishwasher.

Not a minute into their journey, Lisa spotted Laurence and Alice at the bus stop. She was about to say, 'Wave to Daddy and Alice' but her daughter was red in the face and Laurence looked shell-shocked. She couldn't help smiling – at least she wasn't the only one struggling with their daughter.

*

At first, they started the journey in silence, then his mother started asking Max the usual questions. Questions which Max found a chore to answer, were always a chore to answer, to have to construct sentences, inhale, exhale and shape his mouth, lips and throat to say words. Questions that demanded answers when he could be staring out of the window, watching people go past. It was very bright as the sun reflected off puddles still there from yesterday's rain. Max put his palm up to shade his eyes.

'How did you do in the spelling test yesterday?'

'I came fourth, but Mr Carter said that I got all the hard ones right.'

'Have you got your swimming kit?'

'I hate swimming, Mummy.'

‘Do you have it?’

He paused to watch a seagull fly off a bus-stop roof. ‘Yes, it’s in my bag.’

A new chapter in Max’s life had recently emerged, having discovered that if he lied and said he had a verruca, he could get out of swimming. He’d even worked out that he could offer to show said verruca to the sports teacher, and the sports teacher would recoil and say that wasn’t necessary.

He wriggled his toes in his shoes. He could lie and build a reality around the lie which made the lie all the more real. And it wasn’t just any old lie – a silly lie that he hadn’t eaten the last of the biscuits or not-not done his homework. This was a lie that strung his mother, sports teacher and classmates along too. He didn’t know it, but he was learning true deceit.

A part of him felt guilty but really that was just the fear of getting caught and mostly, he was utterly delighted to not have to swim. An idea occurred to him, another brushstroke to paint the picture into reality. He said, ‘I’ve stopped doing widths and now I do lengths.’

‘Well done, darling,’ said Lisa. ‘When I was your age I kept on swallowing the pool water and had to tiptoe to keep my mouth above water. What’s your favourite stroke?’

‘What’s a stroke?’

‘The style of swimming you do.’

He was quiet while he ran through the unique unpleasantness of each individual stroke. ‘I hate backstroke the least.’

‘Because it’s easier to breathe, I bet,’ said his mother.

As her questions got the hint and started drying up, and the car inched through the traffic to school, Max started to feel a little sick as he had done recently on the way to school. Not ill-sick but still nauseous. A small voice in his head taunted him: *You don’t have any friends*. And it was said with that playground melody that goes to 'you-can't-catch-me', sang-shouted by children. *You don't have any friends*. The words were as clear and as loud as if spoken to him, so powerful they arrived as an emotion all of their own. These words tracked him down to the back seat of his mother's car and stayed with him, like a shadow.

He wanted a hug from Mum but if he asked, she would wonder what was wrong. So he stayed in his seat and looked out of the window as they drove along. And anyway, Mo was his friend – his best friend – so it wasn't true what the voice said.

*

When they got to his primary school, he shouted, 'Mo's there!' and the second Lisa parked the car, he jumped out.

'Max!' said his mother after him, and it caught him like a fish hook in the collar. He stopped and turned slowly, his arms hanging down and his eyes rolling, but she wasn't going to let her son dismiss her instinct to nurture.

'Yes, Mum?' he said.

'Kiss?' Her son smiled to himself, taking each step with glee and it grew as he got closer to her sitting behind the open window. When he was by the car she strained against her seatbelt, presented her cheek and he rewarded her with a kiss in the air. Then he was gone into the melee of school uniforms, chaos only kept from spilling out into the world by an eight-foot-high brick wall, iron gate and CCTV.

Replacing Max in Lisa's line of sight was Mr Carter who'd come out of the forecourt, jogging a little to catch her before she pushed the accelerator as school run gave way to commute. He waved at her. 'Lisa?' She pressed the button to lower the window once again and it sank into the door. 'Hello,' he said.

'Hello, Mr Carter, how can I help?' She wondered if he'd been waiting in the courtyard specifically for her. He was wearing a checked shirt and chinos, with a lanyard hanging over his tie.

'I was wondering if you could come in at the end of the day?'

'Do I have detention?' He smiled politely and professionally. She continued, 'What's it about?'

'I'd like to say it's probably nothing but I've noticed Max has gone quiet in class and around the school in general. I wanted to ask if you'd noticed the same thing at home, or if there was anything going on at home?'

Lisa switched off the car engine and leaned an elbow on the door. Firstly, she thought of any arguments at home that might have upset him. She and Laurence rarely argued, mostly because she and Laurence rarely spoke. 'Maybe he's a little quieter than usual, now that I think about it, but nothing specifically. Could there be something going on in the playground? Boys can be quite mean.' She saw her daughter's hard eyes flash before her. 'Well, so can girls.'

'That's my concern. I think it's better if we discuss it in person. We are zero tolerance on bullying but Max is sensitive and the change is stark.'

Lisa ran through the day in her head and scraped together some time. 'I'll come to your classroom at four?'

'I run Chess Club after class. I could sign Max up and we could say five?'

'Five is much better, and yes, please do. I taught Max how to play.'

They exchanged see-you-laters. Behind his teacher, she caught Max's eye through the crowd of pupils and the iron bars of the school gate. He waved at her then vanished. She started the engine and drove away, glancing in the rear-view mirror at Mr Carter who watched her drive off.

Mr Carter was right, Max was sensitive and it pricked her in the chest to think of him quiet at school, sitting at a desk in an empty classroom while other children played outside. It replaced her image of him smiling at his little desk, hand stretched up in the air. Alice would be angry when she heard about the bullying; Laurence, aggressive. He was all their baby.

Was he more quiet than usual? She wanted to say 'no', she hadn't seen any changes in particular, but she presented the plain truth to herself: she didn't know. It begged the question, had she been too busy to notice? As she drove, she thought about asking Laurence to go to the meeting with Mr Carter, reclaiming thirty minutes of her day because she had the executive committee on top of her other work. If she'd dropped everything for each little concern every time she was asked, she wouldn't have had a career.

The change is stark. Surely, Max would have said something to her if he wasn't happy? Surely, she would have noticed?

Chapter 6

When Lisa comes to look back on the meeting she was having then, it will strike her that she should have taken the rest of the week off after her doctor's appointment. It hadn't occurred to her that she might. When looking back on her time in the office, most of these meetings will be indistinguishable from the next and she will conclude that she can't remember them because they weren't that important anyway. But today they were all-important and she sat in the boardroom with the other executives in her company.

'New revenue lines are drying up. We should target new clients in the US and invest there,' someone said.

'The market's hardly saturated here,' said someone else.

The conversation faded into white noise as Lisa remembered sitting on her grandfather's lap. How he smelled a little and the fascinating long hairs that poked out of his nose and ears which she sometimes tried to pull. Would her own parents evoke similar memories for Alice and Max? Thinking of her grandfather reminded her that she'd loved him.

She was thinking of her grandfather because he was the first person that she knew who died. Her parents debated if at six years old she should go to the funeral; they took her in the end. She didn't cry about him then, and it wasn't until she was a teenager that his memory stirred deeper emotions and she had been able to cry for him. She was imagining her own death through the eyes of her son.

Her grandfather had fought in World War II. He taught her how to play chess but forty-odd years later, she wasn't sure she'd imagined it, she would have been too young. It was then that she looked for a tissue in her handbag hanging off the back of her chair and her hand found something it didn't expect – Sara's leaflets, folded and a still a little damp from yesterday's rain.

'So, Lisa can go to the pitch with Adam?'

The mention of her name brought her snap-back into the room. Pairs of eyes focused on her while she replayed the conversation in her head: she was being asked to pitch to a client with Adam. He was stepping on her network, muscling in on revenue.

'Take your time,' said Adam, right in front of the other executives. He gave her the slightest smile, menace only she could see because he only showed it to her. Humiliating. Little. Smirk. *Take your time.*

Caught off guard, the sweat on her skin evaporated into humid air beneath her clothing. This wasn't any other meeting: things were going on that she wasn't picking up on and instinctually, she went on guard. She scanned the executives in a glance, measuring their body language and replaying the tone of their voices in her head. This was not business as usual, or as Jack had said, a 'workflow meeting'. Adam was far further along with whatever he was hatching. Now she concentrated on him, slouching in his chair. 'I'll need to think about it,' she said.

'Well, confirm it before close of business,' said Jack. 'It's a priority.'

Like a flash that stains the eyes, the imprint of what had happened lingered while everyone else moved on to the next item on the agenda. Adam's fingerprints were all over the proposed client pitch.

'Excuse me,' Lisa said. 'I'll catch up from the meeting notes. See everyone later.' Never explain, never apologise and never ask permission.

'Hold on, Lisa,' said Adam. 'Before you leave, I have a question: I got a call from Charlie yesterday. Can I ask why you pushed back a client meeting last minute?'

She stopped collecting her things in front of her and sat back down. 'Okay, Adam. Yes, that's not client protocol. I get it. Can I ask why you were speaking to *my* client? We must look like we're stepping on each other's toes: protocol goes both ways.'

'No, you're misinterpreting me,' said Adam. 'I'm not calling you up for ditching a meeting last minute – even a client one. We've all done that. What I'm asking is why you pushed it back when it was time-sensitive, when you could have asked anyone else in this room to go in your place? They have a tender out.'

'I made a decision: the pitch wasn't ready, and I know my client better than you do. It had to be pushed back.'

Another executive introduced himself into the conversation with a discreet cough, then said, 'I heard that you missed another pitch too. That's not like you, Lisa.'

A third chimed in. 'Bringing these points together, I want to ask straight up: disappearing last minute from the office… keeping clients to yourself… are you interviewing somewhere else?'

'That is a question,' said Jack knocking gently on the boardroom table, 'exclusively for me and/or the board. But as we're here, I can confirm that it was not for an interview.' He looked at her and gave a small nod of support.

'Like I said,' said Lisa, 'I'll catch up from the meeting notes.' She couldn't help the glance she gave Adam and the glare he gave back, his mouth half-open, his eyes following her as she walked around the long table to the glass door.

'Take your time, Lisa, we'll keep you in the loop,' said Adam, changing the substance of her departure, so that 'take your time' meant 'you may go', and now she was retreating from him and the place where men no longer drank whisky and smoked cigars, but they did still carve up the world, or in this case, clients – and the revenue that went with them. She felt the fight stir in her, but she hadn't the energy. She'd deal with him later; she had the ammunition ready.

If Laurence, for instance, had told Lisa to rise above it, she would have retorted that revenue was the basis of the executive remuneration which provided for their family. More than that, it meant a lot being the only woman on the executive committee. Until this meeting, she had been confident of succeeding Jack as CEO, as his closest, most successful executive. So, there was no rising above Adam and what he'd said.

She left the meeting room holding her handbag over her arm with its cargo of three small, folded pieces of glossy paper that would tell her, she imagined, just how sick she was.

Chapter 7

Lisa had privacy in her own office but found herself walking to the closest refuge, a quiet corner of the top floor, the disabled toilet. She turned the handle and locked the door behind her. It had the ambiance of something between a prison cell and a nurse's surgery. White tiles ran up all four walls decorated with Health and Safety notices and handlebars for grip. Later, she would wonder if it was mad to have gone there, as if being in a prison-cum-surgery by choice was a well-known sign of madness, just that perhaps she'd not heard of it.

She leaned into her palms against the tiles and looked down at the floor, as if positioned for a stop-and-search. Adam, Laurence, Max, Alice and Sara. Who next? It was tough to admit, but she wanted to speak to her sister. Not her current sister but the reliable version, the one who'd been so close until recently. The last time they'd seen each other in person, they'd argued and Lisa had said the things that hurt her the most. Of course, she didn't exactly say them directly, just alluded to them, relied on the vulnerable bits of Chloe's life to give meaning to the insult. 'What would you know about making a family and building a home?' That was what she'd said. That's all she'd said.

She was very conscious that they'd only spoken to each other by phone or text over the last six months. They hadn't discussed anything serious, let alone the original argument, or an apology. Instead, they'd gone back to stilted small talk, despite Chloe attempts to initiate deeper conversation. She could be so forceful, so opinionated: familiarity, love and support but with a catch.

The disabled toilet was spacious and eerie. She imagined the other executives still in the boardroom, more free without her, hunched over and conspiratorial. She should have stayed but it had been impossible to do so.

She hung her coat on the peg on the door and put the toilet lid down for a seat, laying out the three leaflets on the tiled floor in front of her like options:

- Leaflet one: Coming to Terms with End of Life
- Leaflet two: Dealing with a Cancer Diagnosis
- Leaflet three: Palliative Care

It seemed right to swap them round so that they became:

- Leaflet one: Dealing with a Cancer Diagnosis
- Leaflet two: Palliative Care
- Leaflet three: Coming to Terms with End of Life

She sat back and looked down at the leaflets. They got smaller the longer she stared at them, obscure pieces of paper with 'NHS' written in the top right-hand corner. She tried to remember the last time she'd held a leaflet. Maybe from a preacher on the street handing them out, or in a tourist office on a sunny holiday. The irony was not lost on her that a holiday or a dose of spiritualism might be useful for someone in her spot.

She took out her phone and started reading news articles but they were about the culture war, each headline buzzing with discord. She wanted to read about the world's oldest dog, or a beaver-reintroduction plan to rewilded Devon; anything to distract her. She put her phone away.

She placed a finger on the leaflet in the middle: Palliative Care. Probably an introduction into what palliative care was because, well... why would healthy people know what it was? She didn't. She pushed the leaflet so it scratched against the dirty floor and when it was at the limit of her reach she left it there, a perfect triangle of NHS support for terminal patients:

- Step 1: Tell them they are sick
- Step 2: Set their expectations for care
- Step 3: Help them to accept death

Was she terminal? Or was it just likely that she was terminal? Or had Sara had something else to tell her before she left, and these leaflets had been given out of context? She took out her phone and googled 'palliative'. 'Relieving symptoms without dealing with the cause of the condition.' Sickness, Care, Death.

The day she fainted – actually, she had used the term 'blacked out' to Sara because it had neither been a hot day, nor had she been doing anything to merit 'fainting' – was now just over two weeks ago. Laurence had labelled it 'passing out', which had irritated her. Had she known subconsciously what was happening in her skull, a tumour dividing and multiplying out of control, eating healthy cells in the middle of her brain tissue? To have said 'blacked out' instead of 'fainted' suggested an inkling prescience.

'We have a choice: we can wait for it to happen again, or I can refer you to a neurologist who will give you a scan.' When Sara had used the word 'neurologist' Lisa had sat up. This was a person with a serious degree – or a series of degrees – that Sara was suggesting a referral to. Because she'd blacked out, once.

Conversely, at the time everything appeared so casual. 'We might as well have a check-up... There's no reason not to... It can't hurt'. All phrases Sara had used which were stepping stones to bring Lisa in for the scan that probably wasn't a one-in-a-million check-up. Being honest, if she'd known it was this serious she might not have seen Sara in the first place. She had been terrified, not for herself but for the children. So terrified that she'd hidden the emotion so that she could get on with life.

It had taken a week after blacking out for Lisa to call Sara who told her, yes, she should come in for an appointment. The first stepping stone that had brought her all the way to the disabled toilet.

Lisa didn't remember stumbling as she stood at the drinks party, or sliding off the chair Laurence had placed her in. She hadn't hit anything in the fall, so it seemed like a case of no harm done. She was more embarrassed that it'd happened in front of everyone. The event filed itself into the 'Anomaly' category, but really that was the 'Don't worry about it' category, which may well have also been the 'Too scary to consider' category. Plus, her husband's report on what had happened was undramatic. Clearly, he had filed it away too.

Laurence had shrugged his shoulders about the whole thing but she did wonder what he'd told his father and handful of friends. 'Oh, you know Lisa,' she imagined him saying, 'always fainting or something like that. She's fine. She's an *ox*!'

Still sitting on the lid of the toilet, she sat up, crossed her legs and folded her arms. She was irritated that he might call her an 'ox' and for suggesting that she fainted regularly, which she did not, even if this scenario was imaginary.

He was her next of kin. A man so distant from her that they could sit in the same room and not have anything to say to each other. And when they did find time together, they stared at the ceiling or talked about her office politics. Next of kin? Not bloody likely. The next! Next to. No one else in between, which was seemingly more and more unlikely.

'It's a one-in-a-million, but we'd better be sure,' Sara had said, and that was the phrase that Lisa had stuck with. *It's a one-in-a-million check-up.* So she'd agreed to carve an afternoon out of her life – of school runs, client meetings, sports days and staring at the ceiling – for a CT scan with a man called Dr Stevens. Bloody hell. She took out her phone and called her sister. Nothing for it.

As soon as she heard the dialling tone, Lisa regretted calling but she stayed on the line because a dropped call would seem so hopeless, only inviting more questions from Chloe. She was angry with her sister, her sister who had no right to call the shots on Lisa's marriage, or still rely on their parents. It was her sister who'd rejected Lisa in so many ways and...

'What do you want? I'm busy.'

The way Chloe said it, as if all one word, the impatience of her tone crumbling in universal certainty that she was not busy at all. What-do-you-want-I'm-busy. It was too much for Lisa, who smiled and, despite herself, felt her eyes tearing up at the same time. Whatdoyouwantimbusy. She held the phone away and took a deep breath.

'Lisa? Is it a bad line? Can you hear me? Fuck's sake.' Chloe shouted down the line as if imitating an old-age trope of one of their parents.

'I'm here,' she said quietly.

'Why are you whispering?'

'I'm in the toilet.'

'You hardly call me, but please don't call me when you're on the toilet. You could at least call me when you have some quality alone time. Or maybe this is that?'

'I'm *in* the toilet, not *on* the toilet. The disabled one so I can speak,' said Lisa. 'I'm not in a cubicle.'

'Why are you calling from there? Have they finally fired you? Mum always says they don't deserve you there.'

Lisa saw the corners of her mouth twitch into a bigger smile in the mirror. It was the sort of thing their mother might have said. The mocking power her sister took – even as an adult, especially as a sister – from their mother's concern and from the impotence of being the subject of a family conversation. Worry was their mother's currency of love, so the daughters had used it, adapted it into a currency of their own based on humour, which they wove into their conversation. It had been years since they'd shared this joke.

'Nothing, I just wanted to speak to you.'

'Oh, bloody hell. Now I am worried. Mum's right – you've been heading for a breakdown for years. Years!' said Chloe. 'Why don't you duck out of work and I'll try and slip past the boss and we can go to the pub for a late lunch?'

It wasn't just a lunch she wanted, her sister wanted a reconciliation. And anyway, she didn't have a boss because she didn't have a job.

'I can't. I've got to pick up Max at school.'

'Lisa, you realise it's been six months since we last saw each other? We don't speak to each other.'

'We are speaking. We speak all the time.'

'We don't *speak*, not about anything real, not since our argument, which requires an apology which I'd like to give you in person. Get Larry to pick Max up. He's your husband, it's what he's for. Let's have lunch.'

*

With Lisa, she had to tread on eggshells, but Chloe hadn't stopped to think before she mentioned the argument, and her heart briefly floated to her mouth. Anyway, her sister knew what she thought about Laurence already: an emotionally unavailable, gaslighting drop-out who wasn't good enough for Lisa.

'Chloe, I can't.'

'Why not?'

'Because I'm a mother, and I have responsibilities.' Her sister's voice was belying something Chloe couldn't quite put her finger on, a message between the lines that needed interpreting, perceptible only to someone who loved her. Was she simply exhausted? Or maybe lonely?

'Well, then, why did you call? It's a desperate cry for help. What's the matter? Can't you remember the last time you laughed? All you mothers are the same. It'll pass, you'll laugh again. When can I see you? I want to see you.'

'You're bored, aren't you,' said Lisa. 'I can tell because you're being more gregarious than usual.'

'It's been a very long time,' Chloe added.

'I can't see you today. Soon, maybe.'

'Are you sure you're okay?'

'I'm fine. Don't worry about me.'

Chloe let silence hang as concern, then broke it off as she recollected, 'How's Alice?'

The conversation she'd had with her niece, which mostly involved listening to her sobs about some boy at school, included moments when Alice had ranted at her mother's coldness. Chloe wanted to smooth their relationship over, but didn't know how. And she felt guilty being between them.

'I don't know. She still hasn't mentioned the break-up to me.'

'Maybe speak to her then. Say I said something vague.'

'No, I mean, she's not saying much to me about anything at the moment.'

'Has she spoken to La-Ree?'

'I assumed *Laurence* was getting on with her better than I was, but I'm not sure. She's a bit like you, you know. Strident, bombastic and clever.'

'Keep going. Don't forget *beautiful*.'

'Except that Alice is more aware of her intelligence than you were at her age.'

'And there was I thinking that we had made it to the end of the conversation without a put-down,' said Chloe. 'At least she's shot of her cheating boyfriend. Some people stay with them.' So much for eggshells.

'Don't,' said Lisa. 'I'm not in the mood.' Then she snapped, 'Life isn't black and white, Chloe.'

'I'm sorry.'

'No, you're not. You say what you want, drop an apology and move on.'

'There's nothing you can do about Alice until she comes to you. Don't intrude like Mum would, you'll just piss her off and get me in trouble. Then she won't be speaking to either of us.'

'Thank you, Chloe. I'll try not to. You know, Alice is very like you when it comes to her temper too. I think it's because she's so bright she finds everyone else irritating. I can see why she went to you.'

'She is like me, isn't she,' Chloe beamed down the phone. 'Bright as a button, my niece.'

An acute feeling came to the fore as Chloe sat on her sofa at home, looking out of her window at the view across town. She imagined her sister in a windowless disabled toilet with a low false ceiling and sanitary bin in the corner, hunched and whispering on the phone as if she were half-imprisoned, half-sectioned. 'Lisa?' But her sister said nothing.

Why would her sister be calling from a disabled toilet, having nothing particular to say? Something was up. Her sister needed her, it was clear, and if that meant some apologies and humble pie, she'd do it. If nothing else, they had to talk through their argument, they were adults now, middle-aged, and that's what adults did. After she had dumped her opinion of Laurence onto Lisa, it had been stupid of her to bring up the 'pond-pushing' incident.

Another long-forgotten resentment stirred now. When Chloe was at primary school, at the end of term she would read her school reports with her parents and Lisa would listen in. If her reports weren't good, Lisa would run upstairs to their father's desk, take out her own report from six years earlier (six years being their age gap), come back and compare them. Lisa had been competitive and nasty to her until one day, when Chloe was eight years old, everything changed.

They were in the park near their home and Chloe said something, she couldn't remember what, possibly about Lisa's growth spurt. Her big sister took one look at her and said, 'How dare you!' the exact tone and pitch still clear in Chloe's memory. Then Lisa pushed her little sister into the duck pond and walked home, leaving her there. It took ten minutes of squelching shoes and sodden clothes to walk home. It was the sound and feeling of shame. She cried all the way but when she got there, their parents hit the roof and Lisa was sent to bed without her dinner while she was taken for a warm bath and given a hot chocolate. The next day, Lisa was nice to her, and the day after that, and the day after that. From that moment on, Lisa had been protective of her little sister, decency burying remorse.

Did Lisa still feel guilty about the episode of the pond? She saw the story in a different light now, her fourteen-year-old sister pushing her little sister into a pond and leaving her there. Who wouldn't feel guilt for that? They'd never spoken about it. All of a sudden, Chloe felt sorry for her sister who didn't have the words to tell her something was wrong, who called from a disabled toilet with nothing to say. The tables had turned and she felt protective of her big sister.

Whatdoyouwantimbusy, but she was never busy and certainly not for her sister, who had been by her side in the decades since then. Lisa wasn't ready to tell her whatever it was that was going on in her life and Chloe wasn't going to put her foot in it by asking again and again. She'd have to wait until her sister was ready. 'I love you. Call me soon, please,' Chloe said.

*

And there it came again, but from a person Lisa hadn't thought could hit her so hard – another view of her new future. Because there would be love left, at the end of their conversation, if she was no longer around. Chloe would still be here but with no one to talk to, no one to relieve her boredom, or with whom she shared sisterly familiarity. To vent petty irritations and listen to her stupid jokes. It was on the tip of her tongue to say, 'I have a tumour. They found something. It's serious. They gave me leaflets about palliative care.' But she said nothing.

Lisa looked around her small prison-cum-surgery and decided that now was the time to get back to work. Adam was taking another client away from her, in broad daylight too. *Take your time.* What a bastard. She needed to speak to Jack before she saw Mr Carter, and in between was a train journey and the drive to Max's school.

She looked down at the three leaflets on the floor, which pulled her away from the phone call, to reality, to facing what had to be faced. There were – with the leaflets laid out on the floor between her and the door – no real life rafts to be had. No school runs, no teenage dramas. So what time she had was precious and the first thing she wanted to do now was end the call. Chloe had cheered her up then annoyed her. So typical. 'I love you too, Chloe. Speak soon.'

'PS! PS. Postscript! PS!' Lisa didn't hang up, but she didn't say anything either, so Chloe continued: 'How much will you pay me not to tell Mum that you called from the disabled toilet?'

'What?'

'It will worry Mum, won't it, you calling me up like this.'

'Lunch when I next see you.' She would be paying anyway.

'Deal.' Then Chloe hung up.

What-do-you-want-I'm-busy.

Lisa glanced at herself in the wheelchair-high mirror and picked out the many facial features she shared with her younger sister. She unlocked the door and went back to her day.

Chapter 8

'I take it that HR spoke to you?' Lisa asked Jack.

'They said you have an ongoing personal matter.'

'Then why didn't you shut down that conversation at the committee meeting earlier? I was under attack.'

'You know why.'

'To show me how on edge the committee is about my leaving the business?'

'No. To show you the current mood among the executives. They're looking for an excuse to carve up your client list. Think, Lisa. You said it yourself yesterday. You're responsible for 30 per cent of the firm's revenue. Some see that as a risk, others see it as an opportunity.'

Once she'd processed what had happened in the committee meeting, the last thing before leaving the office was to see Jack.

'You know that's ridiculous,' she said. 'I'd never call this firm *mine*, but that's how I feel. I've given twenty years of my life to this firm.'

'Oh, it's not just that.' Jack leaned forward. For the first time in a long time, he had shed his overconfident shell. 'It's culture, the words we use. You and I call it a *firm*; they call it a *company*. We work longer hours, we're more ambitious. They are coming after us, you know. They want to take the firm in a different direction, shatter our legacy. I won't let them.'

'Then what do we do?'

'For now, we have to acquiesce. Share some of your clients. Give them the shit ones, who cares.'

'I won't. Adam made this personal. You heard him at the meeting? *Take your time.* You know he's undermining me.'

'Oh, come off it. It's an expression. It doesn't mean anything.'

'It's an expression he uses at specific times. In front of the other executives. When I left for maternity leave. Dozens of times over the years.'

'You're being paranoid.'

'I'm not paranoid. I have eight years of complaints filed on him. Ask HR. I've just never done anything about it because he was never more than a mild irritant – until now.'

'Just share a few of your clients. It makes no difference to your take-home pay.'

'I shouldn't have to and you shouldn't be asking me.'

They sat in silence, neither budging. Lisa wasn't going to concede first. Adam had been her contemporary, joining the same year she did, but she'd been promoted faster. She didn't know who he was until she went on maternity. When she'd formally complained over the following eight years that revenue from her clients – the ones he'd looked after temporarily during her leave – had been allocated to him, she'd never believed that Jack had been the driving force. But now she suspected it was a balancing act, to keep the executives in line to maintain his own position. She saw it clearly: her own career was now being sacrificed for Jack's.

'I need to know you have my back,' she said.

'I could ask the same of you.'

'For god's sake! It's you who's consistently putting him and me together. My clients' revenues were growing before you handed some of them to Adam, so don't tell me I need him. I don't. I didn't need him eight years ago and I don't need him now.'

Jack raised his voice. 'We're not going to rake over the past. We didn't find that Adam or anyone else had been misallocated *your* revenue. We're a business and we collaborate. Especially among the executives.'

She checked her watch. She had to see Mr Carter at 5 p.m. 'I have to go.'

'We'll pick this up on Monday… One last thing.' His tone shifted. 'The personal matter… Everything okay?'

'It's fine, likely nothing.'

'You can always speak to me if you need to, about anything. It's not all *office* between you and me. I think often of how much you were there for me during my divorce. We're a team and we're unstoppable when we're fighting together.'

She smiled at Jack. 'I think you mean *divorces*, plural.'

This was the beginning of the end for them and she knew it. From now, she'd have to start canvassing the other executives and quickly because Adam had such a head start.

Why should she give this place one second more of her time? Because it was her career, her work over decades, and it was being swept from under her feet. She would have to fight just to keep what was already hers.

Jack smiled, leaned back in his chair and waved a hand. 'See you Monday. Have a good weekend.'

Chapter 9

Max enjoyed Chess Club because he won the two games he played that afternoon. Most of the other children were still learning how to play, whereas he and his mother had played quite a lot and he knew simple set pieces. For instance, that afternoon, he'd won a game by putting every other pawn one space ahead of the other, so that they formed an impenetrable zigzag defence, and the other child didn't know how to play against it, sacrificing higher-value pieces just to take one of his pawns. In the second game, he'd castled and kept his king safe while his queen criss-crossed the board picking up his opponent's pieces.

Afterwards, he was tired, but he decided to sign up to Chess Club if he could. Curiosity grew while he waited in the corridor outside the classroom and his mother finished speaking to Mr Carter. It was odd to have her in school, being involved in his domain.

He wasn't even sure if they were talking about him. His best guess was that somehow his mother had found out he'd lied about the verruca. On the other hand, by this point she would have said something to him already, so it probably wasn't that.

He was impatient to get home and hungry for toast. After what seemed to him like a long time, but was less than five minutes, Mr Carter and his mother came out of the classroom and both smiled at him. He stood up and walked over to her and she ran her fingers through his hair. It felt soothing and he knew the school day was over. 'Home time?'

'Yup,' Max said.

'Say goodbye to Mr Carter.'

'Goodbye, sir.'

'Bye, Max,' he said. 'Well done at chess today. You're the man to beat. Have a good weekend and see you on Monday.'

Max pointed out his art on the wall in the hallway to his mother. When they got to the main entrance he looked up to see his mother wave goodbye to Mr Carter, who was still there at the door to his classroom.

In the car, he was more than content to gaze out the window, too tired to speak, watching people in the street. He was sitting in the passenger seat by his mother. He saw a woman taking her dog for a walk. The dog squatted but their car turned a corner before he could see if it was number one or number two.

He wondered if they could make it to ten before they got home – two points for a poo, one for a wee – and started counting. He watched every dog like a hawk as they came into view, straining against his seatbelt to see what would happen. Sadly, by the time they were halfway home, his score was still zero.

Then out of the blue, the universe provided the biggest dog he'd ever seen at the traffic lights. He glanced at the light: red man for the pedestrian, but the car was stuck in traffic. If it was going to happen, now was the time.

'I think that's a Great Dane,' his mother said.

He sat up and watched the dog: it was sniffing a tree trunk near the crossing. It circled once, then twice, forcing the owner to move the lead from one hand to the other. Then it squatted and Max thought he was in line for two points.

When it weed it was such a disappointment, only the one point. Girl-dogs squat for number ones, he realised, as well as twos. It raised a question: 'Mum, what are willies for?'

'Where did that come from? They're for weeing.'

Max thought for a moment: this wasn't the answer he was looking for and he was impatient. 'Yes, I know that. I also know that they're for sex.'

'And do you know what sex is, darling?' his mother countered. Max was silent. He felt stupid.

*

Lisa was asking herself what the right age was to have a birds-and-bees conversation, and decided that a PG version wouldn't do any harm, seeing as her son was asking the questions already. He didn't answer her question, so she continued: 'Sex is the most intimate thing that two people can do physically. And by physically, I mean with their body. Do you know what *intimate* means?' He was silent and, she imagined, in thrall to the discussion of the word 'sex'. She watched him digest the information while the car was stopped in traffic and she didn't need to look at the road.

She continued: 'When we hug, whether that's you and me or two strangers, or Mummy and daddy, it's an expression of intimacy, which is an expression of the emotion between two people.' She paused in case her son had any questions, which he did not. 'Sex is a special hug between two people. It represents two people being together, their emotional context and it's how they make children and can be a way of building upon their love.' She paused to run through something that occurred to her now, something which she hadn't expected to share with her son: 'Sex is complicated and means a lot of different things. I suppose for me, it's an expression of fidelity too. Me and Daddy, or – for example – Aunt Chloe and her boyfriend.' The traffic had moved a little but she continued to look at her eight-year-old boy strapped in next to her, his seatbelt tucked under his little chin. 'If she has a boyfriend, that is.'

'I miss Aunt Chloe,' he said.

'It wasn't that long since you saw her.'

'I don't know, I can't remember.'

Her son shifted between the seatbelt and the seat, and turned away to look out the window again. She put the car into gear and moved off. 'Do you like Mr Carter?'

'Yes, he's okay.'

'And everything's okay at school?'

*

Max heard that voice again, taunting him in its melody – *You don't have any friends* – as if this was the answer his mother was looking for and it presented itself as the answer he should give her. It felt as if the taunt was actually a command that told him to say, 'I don't have any friends, Mummy' and if he said nothing there would be the added shame of not acknowledging what was already shameful.

His bully, Luke, had missed him today. He'd kept his head down, didn't play too much at breaktime, didn't ask too many questions during class. And in the corridor, when he did see Luke, he'd looked down at the floor. It had made him feel lonely, this half-participation in school, but he hated being taunted. Mo, his best friend, was also one of Luke's targets so when he kept his head down, when he didn't ask questions, Mo did too and together they'd kept each other company. Luckily that day, Mo had taken Max's advice and claimed he'd got a verruca too and they spent the swimming period in the classroom, unsupervised, taking turns on his smuggled Nintendo until it ran out of battery.

'Everything's fine, Mum,' he said. 'I'm just tired.'

Chapter 10

The beginning of the end of the day was marked by the punctuation of routine: putting the handbrake on; turning off the engine; unclicking seatbelts; the thud of the front door behind them; the bark from Sebastian; the screech of the chair on the kitchen floor for Max to stand on so he could make toast at the counter; the sound of the fridge opening and closing; and a pot or pan clanking on the hob as Lisa began to make dinner.

Each was a signal for the end of the working day, but also a brushstroke that painted family life. She and Max got home first. She couldn't be bothered to cook a separate dinner for him, so she let him have his toast which he took to the TV room. Butter, or butter and marmite, and one piece with peanut butter and jam, as always. 'It's called a PBJ, Mum.' Then later, they'd have dinner as a family.

Halfway through cooking, she looked down the hall from the kitchen and on the table was her handbag, Sara's leaflets still folded inside. She walked over and checked they were still there.

It made her think of a question: where did the line between privacy and secrecy lie? Not just the line she drew herself, but also the one drawn by her husband. Was it particular for each couple? Or were there objective, reasonable boundaries that dictated privacy within every marriage? For instance, Laurence asked a lot of questions about her work, but she asked almost none about his. She didn't like sharing all the aspects of her life with her husband, but other married people seemed to know about their partner's work. In any case, Laurence would talk about his work without her asking.

The door to the living room was closed and despite Max being in there, no noise came from it. She opened it to find him gaming with the sound off, surreptitiously maximising his screentime. Lisa turned off the Nintendo and set him up at the kitchen table with his homework while she carried on cooking.

When Alice had started eating solids, the nature of cooking changed for Lisa. That extra meal – even if it was a small amount of plain food – took the joy out of it. Before, it had been a pastime, a meditation rather than a requirement to feed her family. Just doing even half the cooking was difficult because she worked longer hours but ultimately put more time into the children. It was only recently that she could rely on Max to eat the same as the rest of the family and not have to cook that extra meal, even if it was fish fingers and peas.

Next home was Laurence. He came into the kitchen, sweaty and panting from a jog. He said he'd have been happy to cook and that he'd do dinner the following night. He suggested they open a bottle of wine because it was Friday night, then went upstairs for a shower.

Lastly, Alice opened the front door with keys clinking and the door thudding shut followed by footsteps running upstairs. Lisa shouted after her that dinner would be in fifteen minutes and she shouted back that she'd come down when it was ready.

Laurence appeared with wet hair and clean clothes, took out a bottle of red wine and poured himself a glass as he began to chat to her about his work. There were two clients who were building ugly extensions to their houses: one would make it look like an old people's home; the other didn't fit with the aesthetics of the original house, and he'd advised that they might not get planning – but they eventually had. He said that there should be more input on the architectural side in the planning process.

It was some time into the story of his day that Lisa asked him if he was going to offer her a glass of wine. She didn't tell him about her workday because he hadn't asked her. After Max finished his homework and went back to the living room, she told Laurence about the suspected bullying at school, but that they'd talk about it properly once Max was in bed.

There wasn't much conversation around the dinner table. Everyone was hungry and tired at the end of the week. Lisa offered Alice a glass of wine and she said she would like one. Laurence stood up and got a wine glass and put it on the table, Lisa poured the wine, a little less than her own glass.

'Thank you,' said Alice.

'If Alice is having wine, can I have a Coke?' said Max.

'Ask your mother,' said Laurence.

'Mum?'

'Ask your father.'

'That's not fair!'

'Okay, then, as it's Friday night,' said Lisa. Max hopped off his chair to the fridge.

'Can you pass me the salad?' asked Alice. Laurence picked up and passed over the salad bowl, made eye contact with Lisa for a moment and gave her a half-smile, a 'here you go' smile, handed over in the same way he handed over the salad to his daughter. Then he went back to his food.

'I'm going out tonight,' their daughter announced.

'Where are you going?' asked Lisa.

'Take your phone out with you and let us know when you'll be back,' said Laurence.

'I won't be later than 1 a.m,' she said.

'That's quite late,' said Lisa.

'It's fine. Don't be later than that, please,' said Laurence, then he turned to his wife. 'How was your day?'

Alice looked her mother dead in the eye and said, 'Thank you, Dad.'

Every day of family life was like building a house from scratch, every beam and brick placed where it needed to go for the children, for the career-balancing act and for the marriage. Moments like this could catch up with Lisa when she least expected them to. But today was different. Today's house had been built over a barrel of gunpowder and as they ate dinner over half-conversations Lisa wondered if she'd strike a match and blow up today's house and maybe the house from yesterday with it too. It dawned on her that she might look back at these days in her forties, each one a house built of family life, and see all she had built was a suburban, dormitory town. And the match she might strike would blow it all up, the whole street.

Over the gentle sound of her family eating dinner, she wanted to shout. She wanted to say to her fuckwitted husband that she deserved some affection and not just because yesterday she'd found out she had a tumour. She deserved affection on the day she discovered she hadn't noticed her own son being bullied for who knew how long; on the day it was made clear to her that she was being squeezed out of her role; and after all of that, she still came home and cooked dinner. She wanted to blow up Laurence's newfound alliance with their daughter that let her go out unreasonably late, and her sister, who had done nothing wrong, but picked up the phone to her niece and found out she'd been cheated on. And she wanted to hold Max tightly and tell him it would be okay.

'Hello? Earth to Lisa? It's your husband speaking. How was your day?' Max laughed along with his father, but Alice was quiet as she watched her parents interact.

'Uneventful,' said Lisa. She gave a generic account of her day that sidestepped Adam, Jack, Chloe and Mr Carter, so that what she had to say didn't take long at all.

'You seem a little tired. No office drama?' asked Laurence.

'All fine,' said Lisa. She would tell him, but not in front of the children. 'How was your day?'

Laurence started to go through his day again, this time in more detail. The last time she'd asked him about his work, Laurence had spoken excitedly about an old cemetery, which needed an archway entrance that would be in keeping with the Gothic aesthetic, and he'd do it pro bono. He liked it, he had said, because it was a unique project. A couple of months went by, and Lisa found herself driving past that same cemetery, and pulled over to look at her husband's work in the flesh. She couldn't find a newly built entrance. It was only after getting back in the car and driving on, that she passed a new gate – an entrance to the funeral parlour. She asked her husband if that was his project and he said, with some dismay, that the project hadn't been – as he thought – for the cemetery itself. In fact, because the land was owned by the council and the construction was being paid for by the funeral parlour, what was meant to be a Gothic stone archway had been rebudgeted to an electric iron gate.

When Laurence finished summing up his day, Lisa said, 'Oh, and I spoke to Chloe earlier,' which she did mostly for Alice's benefit. To remind her daughter that if she could be close to her aunt, she might be close to her mother too.

'The errant sister,' said Laurence. 'Has she found a job, I wonder.'

'Actually, she has a job,' said Alice.

Chapter 11

After dinner, with Max tucked up in bed and Alice out, Laurence and Lisa cleared up dinner together. She asked him why he was being so relaxed about Alice going out until 1 a.m. 'At the least, you could have asked her where she was going?' He replied by saying that their daughter was sensible and had her phone on her. Lisa then told him what Chloe had said, but put it more bluntly: 'Apparently, this boyfriend of hers was cheating with a friend.' Saying this felt like a direct challenge to her husband.

He scratched the left side of his head with his right hand, covering his eyes. 'Oh, dear,' he said.

She asked if he knew why Alice was being particularly bitchy towards her and Laurence replied that it was normal teenager hormones, maybe a mother-daughter thing, he suggested. He said that his instinct was to go with the grain of teenage independence while hers was more cautious – and neither way was wrong. He also didn't rule out that maybe the tension was fundamentally a female thing that he didn't understand.

'What the hell is that supposed to mean?' snapped Lisa. He shrugged his shoulders, and she placed the plates she was carrying back on the table with a bang,

'I wasn't trying to be offensive.'

'Why was our daughter having a go at you at the bus stop?'

Laurence blushed. 'What are you talking about?'

'This morning, I drove past the two of you at the bus stop and you were both red in the face and everyone was looking.'

'Oh, that. That was just her asking for more pocket money.'

'More pocket money?' What bullshit.

'Well, she was asking for a new laptop, and so on and so on.'

Lisa picked up the plates and stacked them in the cupboard. 'That's surprising. I thought we were pretty generous with that sort of thing.' Alice wasn't spoiled, she was grateful for the things she had.

The tension passed as they moved on to Max, speaking quietly in case he came down from his room. According to Mr Carter, he was engaging less and less in the classroom and his grades were dipping. While his teacher hadn't seen anything, he was certain Max was being bullied. In fact, it was because he couldn't see it and didn't know what was going on that gave Mr Carter added concern. 'He thinks Max is suffering in silence,' added Lisa.

'What's Mr Carter like?' asked Laurence.

'Very nice, decent. I'm pleased he's Max's teacher.'

'All teachers are a bit weird, if you ask me. It's a weird thing to want to do.'

'Or you could say,' said Lisa, 'that it's one of the most important jobs in society. Teaching children, who become adults.'

Laurence questioned whether Max seemed unhappy in general or whether his teacher was making a mountain out of a molehill. He offered to talk to his son, but she said now that she'd spoken to his teacher, she might as well speak to Max.

From there, Lisa thought to give an update on the Adam saga but right now she didn't feel like it because Laurence would want to know more and she'd have to be patient as he recollected what he already knew. She'd have to explain the intricacies of the office relationships and then he'd dissect these slowly and offer advice which she didn't want. Lisa sometimes felt her career had become a soap opera to him, one that he had a personal stake in. They took a bar of chocolate and the second half of the bottle of wine into the TV room and watched a movie, but when Laurence went to bed she turned it off and read her book, with a blanket and a cup of herbal tea.

When she came up, he was asleep on his side of the bed but had left the bathroom light on with the door ajar for her to get ready for bed. She dressed into her pyjamas and turned off the light and slid in under the duvet next to him. Usually Lisa felt excited about luxurious sleep at the end of another day but this evening was different.

Out of habit she reached out and squeezed his hand and he squeezed hers back. She'd never asked what this ritual meant to him and didn't think he was even aware of it taking place. He had never asked her either.

She wasn't sure when she drifted off, but she did and that night, she dreamed that she lived in the most suburban street of a dormitory town. In her dream, she had muddy hands and legs from toiling in dirt. The dirt was from her work, burying barrels of gunpowder under each house of this nondescript street.

She dreamed of a warm feeling in her head that grew hotter until it burned like a fuse and she had to run from the houses to stop the gunpowder from going off. But the road turned out to be infinitely long and she ran and ran until she gave up. She went inside one of the houses and it exploded, starting off a chain reaction down the road as each house exploded, one after another.

This was when she woke up. Laurence stirred too. 'Is everything okay?'

'I'm fine. Just a dream. I'm going downstairs for a glass of water.' She took her phone and turned on the torch function.

Downstairs, Sebastian greeted her with his head cocked to one side. Lisa turned on the light and placed the three leaflets from her handbag on the kitchen table.

She read them through once and when she was done, stared blankly into open space. There was no particular information that was essential, nothing urgent in them. The leaflets were there to be read, for people who walked out of their appointment before their doctor could tell them more about their illness. They were simply part of the process of accepting what was happening to her.

She read them again, this time more slowly and cover to cover. They contained little else, but Lisa searched for some hidden resolution inside them, something that might offer tangible aid. But the leaflets did not provide this.

'Look at me, Sebastian, trying to come to terms with my cancer.' The dog looked up at her from his basket, then curled his legs tighter into his body and went back to sleep. She took out her phone and scrolled to Sara's message the night before last:

> *Hi, sorry to text late. I don't want to discuss the results here, but they came through and I've spoken to Dr Stevens and we think you should come in as soon as possible. I've got a spot at 8.15 tomorrow morning. S*

Her response: *The benefit of having a best friend as your family GP! See you then x*

Could Sara just have said, 'The results are serious', or 'I need to see you as a matter of urgency', or just straight up: 'We found a tumour, and it could be cancerous.' Then Lisa wouldn't be rereading leaflets in the middle of the night; then Sara could have been an actual friend when she'd needed her to be.

Lisa went to the counter and boiled the kettle for a tea, cutting up bits of ginger and squeezing half a lemon into a cup. She sat back down to read the leaflets a third time, in the same place Max had done his homework some hours earlier. Sebastian got up and walked over to her, sitting down next to her with begging eyes. She patted her lap and he jumped up.

'You're just a hot water bottle with legs, aren't you.' She wrapped her arms around him. 'That eats, sleeps and sheds hair everywhere.' She kissed the dog on the top of his head. He was a bit like a leaflet, there to help her absorb the worst life could throw at her.

The familiar clanging of keys, the clink of the lock and the thud of the door being shut behind someone interrupted her moment in the kitchen. From the hallway, Alice appeared out of the dark, into the dimly lit kitchen.

Lisa didn't move the leaflets, half daring her daughter to notice a thing that was going on in her mother's life, half daring herself to tell someone.

'Were you waiting up for me?' asked Alice.

Lisa looked for a sway in her daughter's stance or the slightest slur in her speech, but couldn't discern any. 'Actually, I forgot that you were out. I do have other things on my mind than you.'

'Okay, then,' Alice did a sweep of the kitchen with her eyes, passing over the leaflets. 'I'll leave you to think all those things through.'

Her daughter turned to leave but Lisa stopped her.

'Darling, can you sit down for a moment. I feel like we haven't spoken for a very long time.' That wasn't true, they'd spent the day shopping together the week before last, so something must have happened since then. She slid the leaflets off the table and under her thigh. She wanted to ask Alice about her break-up, she wanted to be included. Was it trust that they no longer had between them? Or was it a teenager being a teenager? Was it flippant, or was it fundamental, the distance between her and her daughter?

Alice sat down opposite her, slightly slouched in the chair.

'Have you noticed Max going quiet?' asked Lisa.

'Yes.'

'What do you think it is?'

'I don't know. I've asked him, and he said everything's okay. You and Dad don't get it do you? You say he's sensitive, but it's more than that. He's scared of showing just how sensitive he is. If it's something at school, he'll hide it well. What do you really want to talk about, Mum?'

'I couldn't sleep, so I came downstairs for a cup of herbal tea. Would you like one?'

'I'm quite tired, so... What do you want to talk about?'

'You're angry with me, and I'd like to know why.' Alice sat up, Sebastian looked at one human, then the other.

'You're very distant, Mum. I don't want to criticise your career because it pays for a lot of what we have, but it can't be an excuse for your emotional absence. You need to try harder. It doesn't take a psychiatrist to see that Dad isn't happy.'

Lisa sat back in her own chair. 'That's surprising to hear. My career wasn't a problem last week. Or the week before. I'm not dragging you into my marriage, but it's hard to connect to your father when all I get is literal silence from him, not even words.'

Alice shook her head. 'Don't manipulate me, Mum. I have my own eyes and I'll come to my own conclusions. I want you to treat me like an adult.'

'You don't think he can do anything wrong, do you, although I'm the breadwinner who has to deal with my job being swept from under my feet, and the one who has to pack Max's lunch box too. Not to mention everything else I do for this family. My generation has had to deal with plenty of misogyny but we don't expect it from your generation, and certainly not from our own daughters.'

'I didn't know your job was under threat.'

'We don't need to talk about it, it will be fine.'

'Okay, I get it: a distance is only measurable between two points. Maybe Dad's not trying as hard as he could be. Have you considered how scary it is, to see the cracks growing in our family? Have you considered that from my perspective? Or Max's? Have you even considered that might be why he's gone quiet? You're cold, Mum, and you push us all away.'

'What was your argument at the bus stop about?'

'What argument?'

'This morning, I was driving Max to school, and I saw you two clearly arguing.'

'If you want to know, it was much the same as what we're talking about now.'

Lisa felt like a scapegoat. A scapegoat for everyone in her family and her office and generally, the world. A scapegoat that was also a servant and a punchbag. A servant with a diagnosis, sitting in the kitchen on death row, being told the blame for her failing marriage lay with her and the blame was obvious and factual, as measurable as the distance between two points.

Both Alice and Laurence were lying to her, that much was clear. She matched her daughter's stance: straight back, arms folded. 'Okay, then. Off you go to bed. Stupid me to think I might get empathy out of my teenage daughter.'

'Mum, we can talk about it—'

'I'm not interested in talking about it. You want to be treated like an adult? Welcome to adulthood: people close the door all the time. Go to bed.'

Alice said, 'And there was me thinking it was a defence mechanism, but you enjoy it, don't you – pushing people away.'

In that moment, Lisa didn't notice her own heart rate soaring, adrenaline pumping through her body, but neither did she notice Alice's hands shaking and her lips trembling. She said nothing.

Alice stood up, walked over to the door and said calmly: 'Fuck you, you spiteful bitch. I don't blame Dad.'

'You don't blame your father for what?'

But it was too late, Alice had left the kitchen and a moment later Lisa heard her daughter's footsteps going up the stairs and into her bedroom.

Chapter 12

She scrolled down her contacts to Sara and called, but she didn't pick up on the first or second time. Lisa couldn't imagine a world in which Sara wasn't there for her. She wondered if Sara would look at the name calling and turn off her phone and go back to sleep, hurt that Lisa had stormed out of her office, irritated at her expectation she could call her at this time. But on the third dial, Lisa got through. 'Sorry to wake you up. Your leaflets said I should find someone to talk to, so here I am.'

'Don't worry about the time,' whispered Sara. In the background Lisa heard the sounds of ruffling sheets and muffled voices. 'I'm just pleased you called. Hold on, I'm just getting out of bed.'

'Sorry again to call at this hour.'

'Don't worry. Hold on a sec.'

*

A new, poignant meaning was being crafted to their friendship in this late-night telephone call; one that drew from every moment since Sara had met Lisa at university.

Holding the phone in her hand, connected to Lisa, she felt she was holding the sum of their time together as friends.

All the life experiences – other friends coming and going, boyfriends too, childbirth and wedding vows, qualifications and promotions – shared as pillars on top of which rested this moment.

They had never argued and Sara knew that was down to her patience, not Lisa's. Life had drawn them along different paths. Lisa's was held up between them as the model of a mother and a successful business woman; Sara's path was vocational, the treatment and care of others at its centre. And as time went by, their holidays differed, and their cars and houses, preferences and biases, and finally, their conversation too. But she had always been there for Lisa, perhaps more than Lisa had been there for her, but that didn't matter. Sara held the phone in her hand as she walked out of her own bedroom with her sleeping boyfriend, past her own child's bedroom, and through the corridor to her kitchen.

This was the moment where a million random, incidental things and the far fewer serious decisions in each of their lives were coming together, giving meaning to everything between them. A moment that struck cymbal, sound travelling across their lives then echoing back to a single point in time: right now, this phone call. All built up from the day they met in halls of residence with no clue what was going on, as teenagers studying adult things. It struck Sara that it must have been fate that placed her as the one who gave Lisa her preliminary results. Later on the day Lisa had come to her surgery and after receiving the text from her friend asking for a second opinion, Sara had texted Alice. She hadn't known what to say, so had asked Alice how the rest of the school run was.

Hi Sara! How are you? Sorry we didn't come in to see you. I insisted but Lisa insisted back so we waited in the car. The rest of the school run was uneventful. Why?

Just wondering if you caught the downpour, Sara texted back.

Mum did, I think she went home to change before going into work.

In the kitchen, Sara boiled the kettle. 'So,' she said, 'how was your day?'

'Oh, lovely. Thanks for asking.'

'I tried to call you,' said Sara.

'Sorry, it's not the time for sarcasm. If it wasn't Max, it was Alice or Laurence, or something at work – everything came at once. But nothing's been okay since my best friend told me I had a tumour. How was your day?'

'Not as bad as yours. I got a parking ticket.'

'I read your leaflets. They're useless. Apparently I need to be told that I might be angry or frustrated.'

'They're better than nothing. In fairness, they got you on the phone, didn't they?'

'They did, but Alice calling me a *spiteful bitch* might have had something to do with it too.'

'Wow, *spiteful bitch*,' said Sara. 'They grow up fast and they grow up nasty. What did you do to deserve that one?'

'Nothing. It's teenage angst, wait till yours hits adolescence.'

'From a medical point of view, adolescence is a form of mental illness.'

'I'm going to take Sebastian for a walk.'

'Where are you now?'

'In the kitchen, but I can't stay here. It's like the words *spiteful bitch* are hanging over me. I need some fresh air.'

'Good idea.'

Sara heard a rustle as Lisa put in some earphones and quietly called the dog and sounds that she took as putting on a coat or something like that.

'What were you going to say to me,' said Lisa, 'before I left your surgery?'

'I was going to hug you and tell you I'm sorry.'

'It's that bad, is it?' There was a long pause down the line before Sara heard Lisa's front door opening.

'What do you remember of yesterday morning? After you left my surgery.'

'I don't remember anything. It was raining outside and I stopped in the car park when I saw the children in the car. I got soaked through, standing there.'

'So you don't remember what I said in the appointment?'

'I think you'd better tell me again.'

Sara went over what she had said that morning. 'As a GP, it isn't my area of expertise. From what Dr Stevens said, surgery will be complicated given the location, shape and size of the tumour. There's no point me second-guessing him, so I'll try and speak to him sometime this weekend. And we don't know how aggressive the tumour is, so a prognosis is hard to make right now. I think next step is he'll want to take samples and run tests. How do you feel now?'

'Hold on,' said Lisa. 'I'm just leaving the house.' Sara heard a gentle clunk followed by a rusty creaking noise, which she knew was Lisa's garden gate, as ever unoiled. 'I want to say I'm sorry for walking out of your surgery and that we're having this conversation on the phone. I'm in awe of you wearing both GP and best-friend hats. I don't know how you do it.'

'Neither do I!'

'All the same, I'm sorry it had to be you,' said Lisa.

'I'm glad it was me,' she said.

'But you had to tell me with a stethoscope round your neck sitting on the other side of a desk, when we should have been in my home, on the sofa with a bottle of wine in the fridge.'

She could hear Lisa's footsteps on the pavement. She asked again, 'And how are you feeling?'

'Categorically fine. Psychologically, it hasn't sunk in yet. Physically, I can't feel a thing. No headaches, nothing. It feels like the world is telling me a lie and I'm being told I'm mad because I won't believe it.'

Sara was quiet down the line. By 'world' Lisa meant it felt that Sara had told her a lie. The diagnosis would take time to sink in. Lisa needed to see her neurologist, Dr Stevens, as soon as possible. He had been on holiday and the results were serious enough that Sara had taken the appointment, losing the musical chairs of test results and annual leave. But it was good that the person who had sat in front of Lisa, giving her the initial diagnosis, was someone she knew.

She heard Lisa encouraging Sebastian to move along from a lamp post. 'Do you know how long I've got?'

Sara said, 'I think we shouldn't cast any guesses until we speak to Dr Stevens together. Talking like that is premature. I'll text him now if you want me to.'

'No, don't. Let's be honest, it can wait until Monday. He's a doctor, he needs his holiday.'

'Amen to that.'

The two of them now spoke through silence, the simple language of being on one end of a telephone line at this anointed time. Sara sipped her tea, listening to Lisa's breathing as she walked, both numb to the gravity of the situation, both knowing there was little need to speak.

Out of the silence, Lisa said, 'The corner shop is open. I'm going to buy some cigarettes. I can't see how it'll make things worse.'

'Why not.'

Sara had an image of Lisa, walking around her town at night in pyjamas under an overcoat, cigarette in one hand, dog lead in the other. Down the line, she heard Lisa ask for cigarettes and a lighter. Then she heard a bystander talking in the background.

A minute later, Lisa said, 'Are you still there?'

'Yes. Who was that?'

'A homeless person, I think. He said he'd forgotten his wallet, asked me to pay for his beer.'

'Did you?'

'Yes, I did. And I gave him half my cigarettes. I should have given him the rest, I only want one.'

'Where are you walking to?'

'Towards the little park with the play area. Sebastian's leading the way.'

Lisa changed the subject, and started filling Sara in on the latest chapter in the saga of office life. 'Do you think Adam knows what he's saying, when he says *take your time*?' Lisa asked.

'Don't be so naive,' said Sara. 'Of course he knows what he's doing. Bullies always know what they're doing.'

'Adam's resented me my entire career.'

'Then why don't you leave? Or complain?'

'I won't leave without a fight, and I have complained. I just hope Jack knows what he's doing. That said, I suspect he's switched loyalties too.'

'Who's Jack?'

'The CEO. He's due to retire soon, and I had assumed that I'd be his replacement.'

'Promise me you won't worry about work while you deal with your health.' Sara was treading on the sacred ground of Lisa's work. Catch-ups between the two friends had been getting further apart, although their familiarity was perfectly preserved and typically plentiful when they spoke. Lisa could draw lines in the sand, which she was doing now, by not responding when Sara mentioned her work.

Again, Lisa changed the subject and they talked about the smaller things in life, the things that weren't at the top of their minds but occurred to them only now.

'Where have you got to now?' Sara said, conscious her friend was walking around town so late at night.

'At the park.'

'Is it safe?'

'Well, I'm on a bench, under the streetlamp, so it's not dark.'

She heard the flick of a lighter down the phone line and Lisa sigh as she exhaled her cigarette, then a dull metallic tapping and the sound of pressured air releasing.

'Is that a Coca Cola?'

'Nope, it's a beer.' After a sip of the drink, she added, 'The homeless man offered me one of his cans. Seeing as I paid for them I thought it was the polite thing to accept one.'

'Hold on, I'm going to get a glass of wine,' said Sara. Then a moment later, 'Here we go. Cheers.'

'Good health,' said Lisa.

Sara coughed as the wine went down the wrong way. 'Don't make me laugh when I'm drinking. Anyway, who does that in this day and age, tap a can of beer with their fingernail. You don't see anyone doing it, do you? It's like no one told the Gen-Zers how to stop beer flowing over, and now it's a lost skill. Like map reading or keeping an appointment at a specific place and time.'

'It was our ceremony at university before opening a beer, remember?' said Lisa.

'Of course I do. We had fun, didn't we?'

'Sara?' Lisa paused and Sara felt the poignancy of the moment, waiting for her friend to speak as she found the right words and the strength to say them. 'I want you to be the executor for my will.'

'Won't everything go to Larry in any case?'

'I don't know. I don't think I want that to be the case.'

Sara sighed quietly. 'Lisa, what aren't you telling me?' This was so out of the blue. Lisa and Laurence were solid, she was always saying how great they were as a couple. Was she that out of touch with what was going on in Lisa's life, or was this another line in the sand her friend had drawn without saying anything?

'Can you also make sure I'm cremated? I don't want to be in a coffin.'

'Are we doing this now? Okay then – where shall we spread the ashes?'

'Mix me with water and pour me down the sink. I'll be dead. I won't care.'

'Jesus, Lisa. I'll ask Alice then.'

'I suspect her answer would be the same.'

Sara laughed, 'Why did she call you a spiteful bitch?'

'She's being a teenager. I'm busy with work so I'm not available as much as she wants.' *I don't blame Dad.* 'Of course, I get the blame. Mustn't knock her father off his pedestal, heaven forbid.'

*

Lisa's emotions were churning, ossifying into decisions and she held her watch to her ear and listened to the second hand tick. She had more instructions for Sara but decided they were best for another day, in person. 'I think I'm going to say goodnight and walk Sebastian home,' she said.

'So, I'm meant to leave you smoking and drinking beer on a park bench at 2 a.m., the day after you were diagnosed with a brain tumour?'

'I'll text when I'm home.' They exchanged goodbyes and Lisa promised to call over the weekend when she found a moment.

Chapter 13

Sebastian blinked at Lisa with his head cocked to the side: *What are we still doing here at this random park in the middle of the night?* It was a good question.

'We'll go home in a bit,' said Lisa. The dog stretched out his front legs, then his back legs, first one, then the other. Lisa lit another cigarette and promised herself she'd go home when she finished it.

But time had a way of finding Lisa when she was alone and two cigarettes later she walked over to the bin and threw her empty beer away and put the lead back on the dog. Then she stopped because she saw the homeless man from the 24-hour shop walking towards her. She froze for an instant because the isolated place and hour made a strange man's company unwelcome.

But his slow, shuffling walk and smile reassured her. 'Thank you,' he said, 'for the beers.' He took one out, and opened it without tapping the pull ring. 'Would you like some company?' he asked, sitting down on the other end of the bench. She shook her head and told him she was about to walk back home. 'I think you're my neighbour,' he said, and he confirmed the street name and his number on it.

Lisa hadn't expected that, and was just embarrassed enough to sit back down for what she thought would be a moment, but once she was seated he offered her another beer and without thinking she accepted. They both lit a cigarette as they thought of something to say that was better than small talk.

'You have two children don't you? I see you or your husband shuttling them around every so often. Parenthood is hard work.'

'Yes, Alice and Max.' Lisa imagined him twitching the curtain and recording the world outside. His house wasn't far down the other end of the street. 'Do you have family?' she asked, because a mix of sensitivity and judgement had filtered out the word 'children' from the physical appearance of the man in front of her.

'No, I live alone. And no family either. I have my friends, but life didn't quite pan out as planned. This,' he raised up his beer, 'hasn't helped much.' He looked up at Lisa and shrugged his eyes. 'Sorry, I don't mean to mope.' He lifted up his beer again. 'Cheers, anyway.' Then he took a swig and sighed. 'Can I ask, what brings you to a park bench in the middle of the night?' He spoke a little gruffly, which she assumed was memories dredged up sticking to his throat.

First, she told him that she couldn't sleep, and the dog needed a walk. Then she told him the truth: 'Actually, I found out yesterday that I have a tumour in the middle of my brain. Then I went to my son's school and they told me that he's being bullied, but I hadn't noticed anything. But I see it now: he's gone quiet and I should have seen it. And my daughter hates me and I can't comfort her when she's been dumped by a boyfriend.'

'Christ, I'm sorry,' he said.

Lisa continued. 'There's more. I haven't told my husband, as we struggle to talk much these days and I don't know what to do. I hate the idea of being close to him, but I need his support. I both need it and see it as false.'

The man shifted on the bench. He dropped his fag and stepped on the butt, reached into his pocket and lit another. He glanced up at the night sky like he was saying a prayer, then pulled his overcoat tighter around himself. He looked back down and made eye contact. 'I was bullied quite badly at school,' he said with a smile of misfortune. 'I'm sorry about the tumour. I haven't deserved it, but I've been lucky with my health.'

He sat up straighter and half turned to her. His beer had been going back and forth as he sipped it, but now he held it still in both hands. Tears came to his eyes and fell down his cheek into his stubble, his lower lip trembled. He shook his body, inhaled quickly and exhaled slowly, exorcising an emotion.

'It's okay,' she said. 'It's life. We live our lives with the assumption we're not going to get a tumour.'

'That's not what I'm thinking. What I'm thinking is that now I know why you're here, sitting on a park bench with your dog.' When she gave no guesses he continued: 'Same reason as me – you're alone.' He cleared his throat, stood up and took a drag on his cigarette. 'I'm Bill, by the way.'

'Lisa.'

'Good to meet you, Lisa. Get home safe, and good luck with... Well...' He gave a nod and a kind, happy-sad smile. 'Good luck with everything.'

She watched him shuffle off, carrying the plastic bag of beers in one hand until he turned a corner and disappeared. She hadn't thought of herself as alone. She saw an unopened can of beer that he'd left on the bench. She opened it, took a gulp and lit a cigarette. 'Last one,' she said to a bored-looking Sebastian.

Alone? She had Max and Alice. She had Laurence. She had friends and family and parents and colleagues; a life, a job and a home. She wasn't alone. The suggestion irritated her, especially from a total stranger and – she hated to admit – one that looked like him.

And somewhere in the irritation, in the midst of that emotion, she felt things connect themselves. She felt for her daughter and the heartache she'd confided in her aunt Chloe. She wanted to reach out and explain to Alice that she herself might be being cheated on by Laurence.

She wanted to hug her son and tell him that together, she would help him deal with his bullies, and that he could help her deal with Adam at work.

There was no difference between herself and her children, they were the same being. Their problems made them an extension of herself. She promised that she would not live life on the terms she'd been living it. That in the time she had left, she would leave them with her last efforts on this planet. That in the face of these problems, and with the time left to her, these would be her actions. And in the face of loneliness and death, her children would have this last example from their mother.

She slipped her cigarette butt into the nearly full beer can and dropped it in the bin as she began the walk back home with Sebastian by her side.

Chapter 14

Can you be both in calm waters and in a storm? Can the ocean show a perfectly still reflection and throw crashing waves at you all at once? Can the arrow of time both hit its target and continue sailing through the air?

Because after Friday came a weekend made of all the normal things in family life, one on top of the other until a day in the home was made, done and dusted. The children were one day older, one day wiser. One more day fed, entertained and warm.

Because there was utter stillness when the family ran downstairs or through the kitchen, and each did their own thing or had a parent to drop them off for this or that. Arguments, tiffs, tellings-off, bringing up, dropping off, debates, questions, requests.

And when there was quiet in the house and Lisa was left to herself and time gave her moments alone, there was utter turmoil as her imagination went to work. When words like 'promotion' fell away and new ones like 'chemotherapy' shaped her future.

That weekend Lisa nearly cracked. Exhausted on Saturday and Sunday night, lying in bed next to her husband, she had reached out and held his hand and he held hers – comfort on offer and close by. As if the essence of their relationship was in their fingers and palms, and that was how they knew everything about each other.

But the closer comfort-companionship got, the greater her unease, because the more tightly she held his hand, the more it felt like a gesture. Her husband held her hand each night, but did not come an inch closer and did not come to her side of the bed. He did not whisper 'How are you?' 'How have we grown apart?' or 'What can we do to fix this?'

Would these questions not be easy enough to ask? Would these questions not be obvious to her husband or to anyone watching their marriage from the outside? And would they not say that asking these questions was normal? Instead he held her hand and went to sleep and didn't ask her questions.

As she lay there in bed, she thought that his inaction was not the absence of action but an action in its own right. It was a decision to stay on his side of the bed, a decision to not whisper questions to her and a decision to leave cold space around her, with no words between them. All these things meant that he had decided she should be alone. But still, he held her hand each night.

The instinct to keep him at arm's length was strong and built on emotions she was only just becoming aware of, which were sadness and anger and the humiliation that went with them. There was grief for their marriage too – actually, it was pain – but within this a seed of hope for independence and the essence of herself.

All he had to do was show that he was thinking of her beyond a functioning fucking cog in their family. To ask her questions about how she was and what she was feeling and maybe tell her why he had become so distant. It didn't matter either way: she wanted their intimacy back, that's all it'd take. Then she would tell him.

Keeping the diagnosis and her thoughts to herself was instinctive as much as it was a reaction to him. But it was hard not to stare at Laurence that weekend in the middle of family life. It was hard not to long for the relationship and all the support that went with it and yet sit around a table at meal times, talking. It was hard not to look at him and guess at the truth behind his eyes, all the while reflecting the normality of a weekend with the family. To have something so close and so far. To be in calm waters and a storm all at once.

Chapter 15

Monday morning's school run gave Lisa the sensation of modelling normality and routine, but they were a veneer stretching over her real plans for the day.

She found herself watching Max over his breakfast, following each mouthful of cereal like a story unfolding, because she was looking for apprehension in him as the school day drew closer. She couldn't help offering him more sugary cereal and eggs on toast, both of which he said yes to.

She loved the idea of filling her son's stomach up for his day ahead, even if the practicality of it was often a chore. Every day filling his little engine to learn and work until he came back home tired and hungry for more toast. A simple part of the wider routine, but one for her to enjoy while it lasted.

Spiteful-bitch daughter came down later, and only had time for tea and toast without any butter, which she ate standing up by the counter. She had avoided being alone with her mother all weekend. Years ago, but also seemingly yesterday, she'd sat at the table where Max was, her chin not much higher than the tabletop, munching on bowl after bowl of cereal. Lisa managed not to tell her daughter to sit at the table when she ate and not to say that toast and tea weren't enough for a breakfast. *Spiteful bitch* was still in the air in the kitchen, like dread that hung over the scene of a crime, as if Alice was calling her mother a spiteful bitch every moment they were in there together. 'I'm drinking tea, you spiteful bitch.' 'I'm making crunchy-chewing noises as I eat my toast, you spiteful bitch.'

'Let's not be late,' said Laurence, as he stood up and finished his tea in a pronounced gulp that also said, 'let's not be late'. The children got up and such was the power of routine in that household that both Alice and Max went to say goodbye to their mother with a kiss and a hug and it didn't surprise any of them.

In the hallway, with the kids walking to the car outside, Lisa and Laurence had a moment to themselves. 'I'll be back around five when I pick up the kids, but I'll need to use the study for a couple of hours before dinner.' He stepped closer and gave her a kiss on the lips. The change of tack was noticeable, but she hid the recognition.

'Okay,' she said. 'Have a good day at work. See you later.' She gave him a kiss back.

'You too.' He closed the door with a thud-clang that left Lisa to herself in the house. Moments of tenderness like these were no longer flecks of hope but cause for self-doubt in what she was beginning to realise she would have to confront.

When they were young and working hard and renting separately, Laurence was spontaneous rather than dependable with his affection. When they were newly-weds and new parents, he was dependably irregular rather than spontaneous. Maybe now he was showing her what he could in the only way he knew. Or maybe, she thought, she should trust her instincts rather than question them.

Sebastian had been more or less ignored that morning and wagged his tail when she picked up the lead to give him a quick walk. When they were back, she shook the packet with his dried food and he barked at her until it was in the bowl and the bowl was on the floor. He sniffed at it and saved it for later.

She went upstairs and changed out of her office clothes and into jeans and a t-shirt. She then made coffee and toast for herself, took out a tablet and read the news until it began to irritate her, then read her book. Half an hour later, she made another coffee and checked her emails. There was one from Jack: *Are you coming in today? We need to talk urgently. Life or death stuff. J*

She grimaced at her CEO's amateur dramatics and ignored the email. But it did set off a chain of thought in the back of her mind. Dramatic emails didn't fit with Jack's usual overconfidence. What did she owe to the person who'd taken her under his wing and launched her career? As much as he owed the person who'd done all the hard work for him. Jack's idea, twenty years ago, had been to take their company away from being an industrial manufacturer in the UK and help *other* companies manufacture in the UK and abroad. It was a mix of engineering – designing production lines – and management consultancy. It wasn't earth-shattering work but she was good at it and that was rewarding. They'd done good work together.

In any case, it was a pleasure to ignore him, the icing on a morning taken from every branch of her life and put together for herself and herself alone. One branch from her marriage, one from parenting and another from work.

Just as she was thinking how ironic it was that she could get used to this life, a text message pinged on her phone. She checked, and as expected it was from Sara. It said: *Dr Stevens confirmed he can see us in a couple of hours. We're booked in for 11.30. See you then, there xx*

Her heart raced. But there was hope as today there were few untreatable cancers and she was young and healthy. She rallied her troops for the appointment ahead, but the chairs around the kitchen table were empty and the beds upstairs and the couch in the living room were empty too. The only sound came from Sebastian scratching behind his ear. She wished Sara was collecting her here rather than meeting her there.

Even in a weekend full of family, there had been moments when she'd been able to hide herself away and research online: Cancer Research UK, WebMD, Johns Hopkins, NHS. She read about cutting-edge research programmes, vaccines that targeted the specific genetic mutation in the tumour, immuno-stimulants, and medicines not yet in the public domain.

One article that had stuck in her mind was a trial where everyone on the drug had late-term terminal cancer. The drugs on trial were meant only to extend life but several patients had gone into remission and were now living normal cancer-free lives. She hadn't allowed herself to finish that article because hope seemed so futile and painful. She kept googling these articles and only reading the first half. She noticed it was far easier to read websites about the disease than those about potential cures.

She went to the kitchen counter to make more toast and thought of her daughter standing here, avoiding eye contact with all that antipathy made ridiculous by her school uniform. Lisa consoled herself that this was just part of growing up, but did Alice have to grow up right now?

Her toast popped up and she made a peanut butter and jam sandwich – 'It's called a PBJ, Mum' – with plenty of butter, as per Max's recipe. Then she went back to the sofa, got under her favourite blanket and found herself drifting off so she set an alarm for an hour's time.

Chapter 16

She found Sara in the waiting room, but being in her presence again, she felt embarrassed for having walked out of her surgery and it felt unfair to both have a tumour and be embarrassed but here Sara was, exactly where she needed to be. Lisa was unready for whatever future Dr Stevens cast her, but she was grateful to have her best friend with her.

They hugged and sat down side by side, with a shoulder each resting against the other, continuing the embrace, Sara holding her hand.

'We could be a couple,' said Lisa.

'Or we could be friends,' said Sara without mirroring Lisa's smile, because she knew the appropriate seriousness for a waiting room like this one. Lisa felt slightly admonished and clueless.

'What about your other patients?' asked Lisa.

'You are my patient! My colleagues are taking my appointments where they can.' Lisa imagined the messages on a group chat between Sara and her fellow GPs, whereby the reason she couldn't be at work today was the woman who'd walked out of her surgery, and that woman needed to be taken to the neurologist. The messages she imagined Sara had received back were of support from colleagues who knew first-hand what agony people went through with their health. The generosity to cover one another's workload was humbling because it came from people she had never met, despite having waiting lists of their own. 'Thank you for coming,' she said. 'And thank your colleagues for me too.'

'We cover for each other all the time.' Sara let go of Lisa's hand and put her arm around her.

Lisa rested her head on her friend's shoulder. 'Sorry about Thursday. I hope I didn't scare your patients.'

'Don't worry about them. After you, Thursday was easy: one dose of persistent thrush, a few athletes' feet and a dozen high-blood-pressured octogenarians. Thursday was a walk in the park.'

The arrow of time moved constantly and was sharply pointed, but never was it so slow and so visible as she waited. The clock on the wall was ten minutes slow. It was a large cheap and plastic clock, the sort that took AA batteries and had a dial behind to set the time. It would be easy to correct, she would only have to move the bench, take the clock down from the wall, turn it around – probably blow off the dust collected at the back – and reset the time. It was the sort of thing she would normally do, on behalf of the nurses who hadn't the time to fix it and for the benefit of all the patients coming and going.

Instead, she watched the clock and while she did, she no longer participated in time but sat in a place with a view out on to time, separate from it. She watched the second-hand tick all the way around the face and what she saw stitched together were moments from her life, each one joined up to the present. When there was no more waiting to do, these moments would join up to form a single moment: the one where her whole life flashed before her eyes.

She wondered if this was the speciality clinic in the hospital where she might receive treatment. Aside from the plastic chairs and coffee table with out-of-date magazines, there was a water-and-cup dispenser. The only aesthetic props were two potted plants, in opposite corners, leaves slightly yellow at the edges.

She wondered, if she had told Laurence about the diagnosis, what he would be doing as he waited with her. Would his shoulder be a pillow like Sara's was now? Or would he be pacing up and down with agony on his face, holding grim emotions as his wife fought on? And how authentic would those emotions be? Would he want Sara here or might he be possessive of who should be with his wife as she underwent treatment? She guessed that he would like Sara being there because it would diffuse the pressure on him. He certainly wouldn't want Chloe here, who would rob him of his seriousness by making everything less miserable and he wouldn't laugh at her uplifting jokes or play along with her distracting conversation.

If he were here, he would play the role in an earnest way, but it would still be a role and a face worn because he did not speak to her now, nor ask her questions. He held her hand in a way that played a role too. It would not be with helpless love that he waited in a waiting room, so it would not be what she would want from him.

'Sara?' she whispered.

'Yes?'

'Thank you for coming. Of everyone that could be with me, it should be you.'

The face Sara gave her was difficult to read, but Lisa studied it a moment and thought that her eyes held affection while her brow held concern. She looked at the other patients in the room, avoiding catching their eyes. There was no one trait that could bundle the people in the room together – she broke them down into three categories: the old, the young and everyone else, including herself. The pale hospital lighting and low ceiling made them seem more sick than they probably were, but then again, this was a neurologist's territory, so the lighting might have been aptly reflective. Even the potted plants looked sick.

She stood up and read a poster about concussion pinned to the wall. She walked over to the water fountain, filled up two cones and sat back down giving one to Sara.

A tall, professional-looking man in a shirt, chinos and brown shoes walked through the waiting room and a moment later they were called. Lisa glanced at the plastic clock one last time. It told her they'd been waiting thirty minutes.

Chapter 17

The first thing Lisa remembered – or realised that she'd forgotten – when she walked into his consulting room was how short Dr Stevens was, at barely over five feet. The second thing she noticed was his corporeal souvenirs: a holiday tan and new beard. She couldn't stop glancing at how far the hair stopped from his mouth and she wondered if it was a natural hairline or if he had carefully shaved the effect, which was to make him look odd.

'Lisa, it's good to see you again and I am sorry about the circumstances. Please, have a seat. Hello, Sara.'

'Do you know each other well?' asked Lisa.

'Yes, she referred you directly to me, but,' – he smiled at Sara – 'she's been referring patients to me for nearly a decade. So this,' Dr Stevens opened his palm to the tall, professional-looking man who had walked through the waiting room and now sat to the side of the desk, 'is Dr Obi Okoye, my recommendation as your oncologist.'

She shook Dr Okoye's hand and considered for a moment that all these people were here just for her. Her at the centre of events, her on the table.

'So,' he continued, 'let's recap, shall we? Three weeks or so ago, you fainted – *blacked out* I think was the term you used to Sara, when you saw her a week after the event. On more or less a hunch – but specifically, as you felt uneasy about blacking out without there being an obvious reason, such as a hot day or a head rush – you agreed to a CT scan rather than waiting to see if you'd get another blackout.'

'That's correct,' said Sara.

'To be clear, there are and have not been any other symptoms, persistent or passing. No headaches? Nausea or dizziness? Tiredness that can't be explained?'

'Generally, I'm tired between work and family. But no, none of these things.'

'How do you feel today?'

'I feel confused, like this is all so abstract and intangible. I walked out of Sara's surgery when she told me that you'd found a tumour.' Describing her own transgression felt like a kindness to herself because she was admitting that she was in shock and accepting that it was okay to be in shock.

'It can be like that. We'll come back to the psychological aspects of your situation shortly. So, after your initial appointment with Sara, you saw me and a week after that we performed the scan. But I then went on holiday. Having reviewed the scan while on holiday, I deemed the matter urgent enough for Sara to liaise and tell you the results immediately. That was five days ago – last Thursday. Can you tell me what you understand of the diagnosis?'

Dr Stevens used the word 'the', not 'your' diagnosis and she felt he was talking about a tumour, not *her* tumour and a potentially terminal illness – not *hers*.

'Well,' she glanced at Sara to corroborate, 'I have inoperable, terminal brain cancer and—'

'Let me stop you there. You almost certainly have cancer, but there is a chance the tumour is benign – that's where Dr Okoye comes in. And it is almost certainly inoperable. But that will depend on whether the tumour cells are distinguishable from healthy brain tissue when we have a closer look with an MRI and biopsy. But even if it is distinguishable, it looks likely from the CT scan that we will not be able to remove all of it. The tumour has a centre, but has expanded out in roots rather than grown as a ball.' The doctor used a fist and fingers as a graphic aid to demonstrate the shape of the tumour. 'And given its location, that makes surgery risky. What else did Sara tell you?'

'That's it. I'd like to know about timing – do I have months or years?' Lisa felt like a child sitting in an adult's chair and it reminded her of Max in the back seat of the car as his legs dangled, gently kicking the driving seat. The more time the doctor took away from her, the smaller she felt.

'Again, I should clarify. Such is the development of the tumour, I wanted Sara to see you immediately. Symptoms could increase dramatically at any moment. On the other hand, if it's not cancerous, if it has very slow growth, you may have years. This tumour may have been growing for some time, we don't know yet. My educated guess – but nevertheless I emphasise that it is a *guess* – is that you have between six and nine months.'

'For clarity,' said Lisa, reflecting her neurologist's officiousness back at him, 'that's months before I die?'

'Yes. In the meantime, you may lose particular functions of the brain. Anything from vocabulary to bowel movement. The brain is extremely complex; it'll be hard to predict how the tumour will affect it.'

Lisa had not thought of side effects. In moments when her imagination had taken liberties over the weekend, it had been to indulge in eulogies and graveside tears, but now she realised she had jumped straight to death without considering the process of dying first. She imagined herself using disabled toilets and stuck in a wheelchair at home. The lack of independence terrified her.

Sara now took up the mantle of optimism on Lisa's behalf because she herself was unable to muster any against the cold science landing on her from Dr Stevens. 'What about cutting-edge medicines?' said Sara. 'Gene therapy? mRNA vaccinations? Are they an option? Drug trials?'

He turned to her, 'Pre-emptively, I have already been in touch with three professors I know running trials in the pharmaceutical industry. Two couldn't consider your case on the grounds that the tumour is so developed. Places are limited and a patient at this stage of tumour growth may skew results. The third – Dr Okoye's contact – will need to see a biopsy report, to see if it's the right type of cancer for the drug they're testing.' He turned to his patient. 'Lisa, even with advances in modern medicine, if this tumour is what I expect it to be, a glioblastoma, the chances of remission are small. I must caution you not to get your hopes up.'

'Don't worry,' Lisa said, 'there's no chance of that. I get it: no miracles. Just lie back and wait.'

The doctor looked at his colleague, then to Sara and Lisa for consensus. 'The thing is, Lisa, you already are a miracle. If I had only seen your scan, I would have said with reasonable confidence that you had likely already lost some mobility, or had another such symptom.'

'So what you're saying is that every moment is precious.'

'Very much so.'

The absolute nature of what he was saying filled the room. 'Is there absolutely no chance of surgery?' said Sara.

'Here, you get to a question of quality of life. To be anything like sure that we'd be prolonging life, we'd have to be thorough in surgery. This would likely mean removal of healthy tissue too, and that's on the assumption it's clearly distinguishable. But that could result in side effects similar to the symptoms. The brain is the material that makes you *you*.'

Dr Okoye spoke for the first time: 'I've reviewed your medical history. You're in good health otherwise, so I am hopeful for identifying an effective treatment, where effective means life-prolonging. The next step is the more detailed MRI Dr Stevens mentioned, along with a biopsy. This will give us much more information about what we're dealing with. I'd like to get you in as soon as possible for both. And until we do, I recommend setting aside all assumptions.' He glanced at Dr Stevens. 'Guesses aren't helpful at this stage.'

The first thought that went through Lisa's mind wasn't fear of the biopsy procedure, or even of the results from it, although later she would wonder why it hadn't been. The first thing she thought was what excuse she would have to make if she had to stay in hospital overnight. Could she say she was visiting her parents? What would the bandage look like? When would she have to tell her children? Soon, there would be no choice but to tell them.

Her imagination played a sudden trick on her, of a different scenario, where it was not her, but one of her children who had a tumour in their skull and that she was in Sara's role and that Drs Okoye and Stevens were paediatricians. In this scenario her role was to care for them through any procedure, for however long it took and at any sacrifice.

Next she thought of her own parents, who would not want to be anywhere else other than by her side. They would want to be in this tiny consulting room, crowding it out beyond capacity, cradling her. She would be surrounded with support.

And then in her mind, she was a child and it wasn't Max or Alice with the tumour, but herself, thirty-something years ago and her own mother was in Sara's place, looking down at Lisa giving her a brave smile.

Lisa looked back at the two doctors looking at her and struck these scenarios from her mind. The doctors were here for her, not her children, and they were here for her now, not when she was a child. She was not a child. Now, she had a family of her own.

'What does a biopsy involve?' she asked Dr Okoye. 'And when would you like to do it?'

Chapter 18

As the appointment went on, Sara kept glancing at Lisa. They had, once, crashed a car. It was the year after they left university and Lisa was driving and they joked and laughed and cheered each other up as they waited for the breakdown crew, ambulance and police car. It was only when the paramedic gave them blankets that Sara realised they were both shaking uncontrollably.

The problem with specialists like Dr Stevens was that they became immune to the gravity of their field within medicine. If Dr Stevens was having conversations like this every day – and being a neurologist he probably was – then getting patients to fully and quickly understand what was going on with their health was essential. As a GP, Sara was close to the opposite of this and the contrast was heart-breaking because while this was fact and science, it was also life and death and the emotions that went with them.

She didn't know how Lisa would react. At times she could be capricious and mercurial and now she thought about it, she should have expected that Lisa might walk out of her surgery and back to the school run.

Lisa began to shiver and the colour from her face faded, Sara stopped the doctors speaking. As her friend started to break down, the two doctors picked her up with their shoulders under her arms like a survivor of a mining accident pulled from the earth, who hadn't the strength to walk. They took her to the room next door and placed her gently onto a sofa. Dr Stevens took Sara aside and told her she could take as long as they needed in here. He asked her to knock on his door before they left.

The doctors left them alone and Sara joined Lisa on the sofa, slipping an arm around her. The room was small, tiny, almost impractical for any use other than maybe storage, but squeezed into it was the sofa the width of the room, a small coffee table and another small chair. The chair was for the doctor and the sofa for the patients.

Sara had experience of rooms like this. Dotted up and down the country, in hospitals, surgeries and clinics. Counselling rooms where consultants and nurses took patients and bereaved relatives and other people in crisis.

Sara had witnessed more emotions in rooms like this than anywhere else on earth, memories that never went away. Staring at the chair from the sofa, she was acutely reminded that today her role was reversed.

She hadn't seen Lisa so helpless since their car crash. 'Do you want a cup of tea?' she asked, and her friend gave a gentle nod. 'I won't be long. I'll be just outside.'

Sara walked out into the corridor busy with health-care professionals and found the coffee station in a room not far from Lisa. A nurse said, 'You're not meant to be in here.' Sara took out her NHS ID and said she wouldn't be a minute and that she was making a cup for a friend. The nurse went back to ignoring her.

She put the kettle on, found two mugs in the sink and washed them up. She thought sugar would be good for morale, but knew Lisa didn't take it. So, she made one with and one without, throwing the teabags into the bin and walking back slowly so as not to spill.

She turned the doorhandle to the counselling room with her elbow and pushed the door with her hip, hearing as she entered a distant voice say, 'Lisa? What's wrong? Where are you? Hold on, let me get your mother.'

Lisa was holding a phone next to her ear, her teeth chattering and eyes unfocused. Her breathing was erratic too and Sara suspected Lisa was some way in to a panic attack.

Sara put the teas down on the table, took the phone off her friend without asking, encountering no resistance. She looked down at the phone which said 'Mum and Dad Home'. 'Dan? Cath?' Sara spoke into the phone. 'It's Sara, Lisa's friend.'

It was Dan who spoke, 'Sara, what on earth is going on? Is Lisa okay?'

Chapter 19

Sara drove Lisa's car to her parents' house, about half an hour from the hospital. It had been many years since Sara had been to Lisa's childhood home, which made it a journey back in time as much as a journey to a place. Within a couple of minutes the motion of the car rocked her friend to sleep and at a traffic light, Sara pressed a button to warm each front seat and reached behind to grab a coat, which she tucked gently around Lisa. She thought about putting the radio on quietly, but decided that silence would be more restful.

When Sara had spoken to Dan and Cath on the phone she'd not wanted to explain too much, reckoning Lisa should tell them in person. Lisa could be fiercely private, and given she'd walked out of her surgery, Sara didn't want to risk alienating herself when she needed to be close to her friend. Sara handled the call with Dan delicately, but didn't want to create unnecessary stress and paranoia for Lisa's parents by withholding information – the thin line she'd often been left to tread in their friendship. Right now, urgently, she needed Lisa's confidence as she helped her to find the support she needed, which begged a further question: why-oh-why wasn't she telling Laurence?

After the call with Dan, she waited until Lisa caught her breath and was ready to speak. Sara had discussed getting a second opinion, to which Lisa gave a dismissive frown. What was the point of a second opinion? she'd asked.

'Lisa, even Dr Okoye said you need another opinion from another neurosurgeon,' she had said, but Lisa looked confused, as if she'd not been in the same consulting room a moment before. 'Parts of the tumour may be easily removable once a more detailed MRI comes back,' Sara had continued. 'And when Dr Okoye has the pathology report in hand they can identify the best course of chemo and radiotherapy. There are still options.'

From what little Sara knew of this area of medicine, there was hope, but her friend had to find the resolve to undergo the treatments. The cancer might not be aggressive, or they might identify effective treatments which could mean years more life, even remission. Lisa had a stubborn nature, which Sara knew from a thousand blunt comments over the years. It came down to this: she feared that Lisa might choose quality of life in the time she had left, rather than treatment and side effects and years of struggle. Dr Stevens had been so exact as to be terse – unhelpfully so.

Sara had waited in silence for Lisa to finish the tea in the counselling room. Then she said, 'I promised I'd take you home.'

'What did you tell my parents?'

'I said that you've had a serious diagnosis and that you need to speak to them. They asked me where you were, and I said hospital. They said they'd come, but I said you weren't an inpatient and that we'd go to them.'

Throughout their friendship, Lisa had not taken one role but many as she evolved. She had been the lazy student, the work-hard-play-hard graduate employee, the funny one on nights out, the serious one who cancelled plans to stay in the office, the intelligent one who suffered no fools, and so on. As life unfurled, she became the overworked one, the stressful one, the dismissive one, the snobbish one and the one who was hard to track down and reach out to. Now, she was the one who needed help.

Burning away all weekend was why Lisa had asked her to be an executor to her will. Sara wasn't a lawyer, but as she understood it, Larry would automatically inherit Lisa's assets. Maybe the request was a formality, a sort of recognition of Sara's friendship, like being a godparent but for your estate rather than your child. Lisa had never mentioned anything, and it hurt her that she might have felt unable to confide in her.

Sara wanted to call Laurence on the car phone and ask him directly what was going on, talking in whispers while Lisa slept next to her. She started to imagine the conversation with Larry, but as it was, she arrived at Dan and Cath's and parked the car, putting a hand on Lisa's shoulder. 'We're here,' she said.

Lisa came round slowly. 'How long was I out?'

'Pretty much the whole way.'

They unclicked seatbelts and walked through the front garden. 'Ready?' asked Sara and Lisa nodded, the sleep still lifting off her. She knocked on the door and a moment later Dan invited them in. They walked through to the kitchen to Cath, who had blotches around puffy eyes.

'Have you had lunch? Sara, can we interest you in some shepherd's pie?' asked Dan.

It was so out of the blue, so far from her mind that she laughed. 'I'm fine thanks, Dan. I've actually eaten. I was thinking that I'd go for a walk and leave you three to it.'

'Good idea. Follow me,' he said and Sara followed his squeaky trainers to the front door, through their little front garden and back onto the street. He stood there, shifting from foot to foot. 'Thank you for going to the hospital. You've been an extraordinarily good friend over the years.' Then his back straightened. 'Right, follow our street until you see a field. There's a gate and that leads you to a National Trust pathway. Every fork you come to, take a left and you'll end up the other end of our street. The whole walk takes about forty-five minutes, or less for you because you are young.'

'Thank you.' She wanted to say something comforting but couldn't think of anything that didn't sound like a condolence. 'I've always got my phone if I get lost. See you in a bit.' On the walk, she thought about Max and Alice and how she could help Lisa's family. Her own daughter was between them in age, but she could offer to do fun things with Max when Lisa needed. She was also Alice's godmother, although no one was religious and there'd been no christening. She imagined herself as a surrogate mother, along with Chloe, at Alice's life events. Maybe Lisa might become religious now. In her head, Lisa said, 'Well of course religion would be fucking useful; it basically exists for death. Religion is death.' Sara smiled at her friend's blunt pragmatism.

She finished her walk and waited in the car. The house Lisa grew up in was beautiful and had moss on the roof tiles, but also clean, white-painted window frames. The walls were made of flint, with red brick at the corners and around the front door and windows. Despite their age, Dan and Cath were clearly still working at their garden and it showed all the signs of spring, growth in an orderly fashion belying their efforts.

The house looked calm and beautiful, loved and well lived in and Sara wondered how the conversation was being had around the kitchen table, and how the pain and sadness would play out.

When she and Lisa were younger, visiting this house had been exciting and Sara learned more about that part of England where everything was a little bit more formal and traditional. Sara's own father had emigrated to the United Kingdom in the eighties to be an NHS doctor. The invitations to Lisa's home had been a window into not only a family but much of Britain.

Around an hour later, Lisa walked through her parents' front garden and climbed back into the car. She made to give her friend a hug, but rested her hand on Sara's forearm, as if thinking better of it.

'How was that?'

'I hadn't given them a second thought. I'd just been thinking of the kids. I feel like I should spend every second that I have with them. Let Mum fuss and Dad worry but...'

'But the kids?'

'But the kids.'

Lisa looked in the glove compartment and found a tissue to blow her nose into. 'They've made me promise to tell Chloe this week, which will be a hassle. She'll want to tell me what treatments I have to undergo, or that I've got to go on safari or go to Glastonbury before I die.' The sky began to darken again and clouds seemed to hang lower. 'I'm worried how Chloe will take the news.'

'You're always worried about your little sister. Focus on yourself and your family.'

'I need to get to the supermarket before the kids are back from school.'

'You can forget the bloody weekly shop for one day. Can't you do it online?' Sara started the ignition and moved off. 'What did you tell your parents?'

'I told them I had cancer and it was probably terminal and that the doctor's best guess was that I had between six and nine months. I didn't tell them about Dr Okoye and more tests. I wanted to keep it simple and if something changes, I'll let them know.'

'That seems sensible: tell your parents there's no hope and surprise them when you make it to Christmas. I know you, Lisa: you're not telling them about possible treatments because you know they'll put pressure on you to take them.' Exasperated, she wanted to pull over.

She could see Lisa glaring at her from the corner of her eye as she looked forward at the car in front. Sara continued, 'While I've got you in the car, you should hear it from me. Any one doctor can be wrong, and even though I don't think Dr Stevens is wrong, he's painted a very absolutist picture and that may have given you the impression that it would be heroic to forego treatment and enjoy your life while you can. Whether you have treatment or not, you will have to fight each symptom as it arises. And Dr Okoye could come back with results showing that the tumour is benign. Or the MRI could reveal that large chunks of it are operable. Or there may be effective new treatments.'

'I'm at my daily limit of discussing my health. What I heard from Dr Stevens is that I am already lucky to be alive and what you're saying now is that I should be hopeful on top of that. I think it would be a total headfuck to start going through all the ways I can be hopeful.'

'I don't want you resigning your life away, that's all.'

'By *resigning*, do you mean succumbing to a tumour growing in my head? And by *hope* do you mean undergoing incredibly painful chemo and radiotherapy which, in the end, might not extend my life much at all?'

'Um-hm.' Sara waited a little longer, then said, 'And also, while I've got you here...'

'I haven't got the strength to speak anymore, driving along the A-whatever-the-fucking-road-we're-on.'

Lisa switched the radio on, already tuned into a local station which played rock music. They listened until the end of the song then the DJ spoke for a bit about a competition the station was running and introduced another song, by Blondie. When it was finished, Sara turned off the radio.

'No, we can't leave it there, because I don't know when I'll see you next,' said Sara. 'So, here it is – what's going on with Laurence?'

For a good while, the only sound in the car was from the engine and the wheels on the tarmac. Sara could see Lisa out of the corner of her eye staring back at her and she readied for her to snap. If Lisa was considering changing her will, there was a more serious issue at heart: that she wouldn't be able to rely on her husband right when she'd need him the most. Not just for emotional support, but potentially the physicality of care as symptoms arose.

At last, Lisa sighed and said, 'Sara, I owe you an apology.'

Sara glanced over and saw her friend's expression had softened. 'Why? What do you mean?'

'Laurence and I have been growing apart for a long time. I made a very conscious decision to confide in only one person, and that person was Chloe and for a long time that was okay, and I could deal with it like that, speaking to her, but then the niggles started piling up and one day she cracked and said that she was just enabling me and my marriage. We had a massive argument in a coffee shop and we haven't spoken to each other since. At least, not in person.'

'I thought you and Laurence had always been solid.'

'We only really talk about two things: work and the children. That's pretty much it. There's no intimacy.'

'Do you think it's fixable? What are the niggles?'

'Stupid things that are probably my mind playing tricks.

A couple of years ago he started taking an interest in his appearance, took up jogging and lost a little weight. I thought it was for my benefit at first, but our sex life fell off a cliff. Then he started going to architectural conventions out of the blue. One time, he had changed the sheets on the bed and said he'd spilt coffee. Lots of really little stupid things that I've dismissed, but Chloe told me to confront him and I just didn't want to deal with it. You know how life is and she just doesn't get it.'

'But why couldn't you speak to me?'

'I wanted to, but the whole thing with Chloe made me feel trapped. So I didn't say anything else to anyone. I'm sorry I kept this from you.'

Sara felt more excluded than usual from her friend's life but at the same time she knew that it was not the time to put her feelings forward. She asked, 'Do you think you and Laurence can work it out? With everything else going on, with the tumour and everything you told me that's happening at work, I think you need all the support you can get.'

'I don't know,' Lisa's voice cracked. 'I don't know. I don't know. I don't know.'

Chapter 20

Lisa watched Sara wipe away tears with her sleeve, one hand on the wheel, first left sleeve to left cheek, then right sleeve to right cheek. 'You know I'm here for you. Whatever you need,' said Sara.

Her mind cast back to reality, and in front of Lisa was the weekly shop on what would normally be her way back from work. Laurence worked from home and would pick up Max – sometimes Alice too – but later they'd all be home, and they'd all be hungry.

They pulled up next to Sara's car in the hospital car park and hugged goodbye. And as she told Sara about the state of her marriage, Lisa was all too aware of the betrayal in not telling her friend sooner, her guilt for painting a picture of domestic bliss. After Chloe's reaction, and the argument that had followed, Lisa had decided to tell no one else, because she'd expected Sara to have suggestions or explanations, or advice on what to do, or that she might play devil's advocate that there was something that might explain his behaviour. Instead, Sara just hugged her at the end of the car journey, showing she had support when she needed it. They made a plan to meet the day of the biopsy results which was a few days from now, at Dr Okoye's office.

'Sara, I forgot to mention something.'

'Yes?'

'My father is willing to be an executor, if it's still uncomfortable for you.'

Rain began to hit the screen and Sara handed the key back to Lisa. 'That's okay. I'll do it.'

'Thank you. Dad's nearly eighty, I didn't want him to have to go through my estate after he's buried his daughter.'

'I thought you wanted to be poured down the sink?'

Lisa smirked back. 'I won't mind much either way! I'll be dead!'

'What are you going to do about Larry?'

'I don't know yet. I made Mum and Dad promise not to speak to him about the cancer. I think Dad cottoned on to something, and I could see it made Mum worry more.'

'I think you need to confront him – either have his support or draw a line under him.'

'If only it were that easy. He's part of my life, he's the children's father. He'll be here after I'm gone and I do still love him.'

'I know, it's not easy. Dealing with it won't be easy.'

'Sara, I feel I owe you an apology. I haven't treated you as the friend you are. You were there for me at 1 a.m. on Friday night and you've been here for me today. If it weren't for you, I'd be in the office or doing the school run or whatever else needed doing until I blacked out again, unable to lie anymore.'

'Lisa, of course I'm here.'

Chapter 21

After the morning with Sara and the afternoon with her parents, Lisa found refuge in the routine of the weekly shop, albeit a dull necessity. Her family would still need the weekly shop, with or without her. Typically, the shop was split between her and Laurence alternating each week, like the school run each day. It was a necessity, so it was done.

Lisa walked up the aisle of the supermarket along with every other mother and every other father, and every person that fed themselves because everyone ate. Except today there was a new distinction: she was eating until she died and they were eating so they continued to live. It was an upsetting thought – her vs. everyone else – that made her a little angry because everyone else was taking their weekly shop for granted.

For example, if six months really was her lot, if six months more was all she was getting on this planet, why should she spend another second in the supermarket, on these domestic things? But it also occurred to her that if she told her family that she was sick someone would still be doing the shopping and while she was still able to, that would still be her, every other week.

She felt clamped down by these serious doctors who knew about tumours and had set about convincing her that their diagnosis was real. Maybe, if she refused to believe them, they'd put her in a straitjacket. Men in white coats would come and get her, insisting on her fate by reading out the test results like a judge read out a sentence in court, as she was dragged away to an asylum.

She wanted to launch her shopping trolley at the other shoppers, throw it against them and scream, 'Keep your fucking weekly shop, and have my fucking tumour while you're at it. I want to—'

Want to what? Live longer? Like when they said, 'Live a little' and this was her time to live because she had so little life left. She preferred 'Live a little longer', or even: 'Live longer, full stop'.

Life – Lisa's life – which at the beginning had had decades upon decades to spare was all of a sudden only happening once. 'Blink and you'll miss it,' someone old said to her when she was young. Time seemed less expensive when she was younger, but it wasn't. It was just easier to spend. Now every moment was precious and yet she was in a supermarket. It was as if life was supposed to happen many times over, but now it would only be happening once, or in fact, it had already happened.

What should she do about work? She wanted to walk away from it. Between the fruit and veg aisle and the dairy aisle, between trying to remember which yoghurts everyone in the family wanted and which vegetables they needed, she turned on her phone. Several texts pinged in and she realised it had been off since she'd called her parents from the consulting room. Within a moment Jack rang from another universe.

Life and death stuff – that's what his email had said this morning. What were the chances he happened to call just as she turned on her phone? How many times had he rung her already? She looked down at the screen, which was dispelling its rage through high-pitched vibrations and the name on the screen: *Jack Office.*

In between her hospital appointments and her husband and her parents sick with worry and her friend cornering her in the car asking about her marriage and the weekly shop and her tumour; in between all these things was Jack forcing her to share her clients with Adam. Why did she have to deal with this shit? The answer was she didn't, so she sent his call to voicemail and it felt good to frustrate the vibrating phone. Almost immediately, she saw a message from him: *Please call me back.* On autopilot, she opened her email, and saw one entitled: *Call me asap.* She was done with him. He had stabbed her in the back and her only regret was not seeing it years earlier.

She stopped in the middle of the aisle because her legs were unable to move. The shoppers around her continued to take items and place them in their baskets and trollies, as if everything in the world was perfectly normal and nothing else was going on. They stepped around her and didn't pay her any attention. Her legs wouldn't move even though she begged them to. She wanted to climb into her trolley and ask one of the shoppers to push her around the supermarket. Not far, just to the exit.

Her phone vibrated again and she looked at a message from Laurence: *Picked up Max and spoke to Mr Carter about the bullying. See you later. x PS. Max says he finished the Coco Pops.*

The first thing she felt was an ice-cold wind that started at her feet and crept further up her body, through legs and torso. It stopped at her neck and she hunched her shoulders as the cold sank in and her body shivered. She wished she was in bed like a sick person should be. The cold turned to heat around her neck and it felt like the blow from a hairdryer. It ran down her skin, over her chest, her stomach, her waist and all the way to her feet. She could feel her skin blush from the temperature with cool sweat in odd patches.

Her legs let go of their grip and she started to walk again as if nothing had happened. What was that? Perhaps the tumour was affecting her body? She found herself by the cereal aisle confronted by the familiar, well-trodden dilemma of Coco Pops or Rice Krispies. Within this dilemma was a divide that separated each half of their marriage.

She took the Rice Krispies from the shelf and put it in the trolley, but she also thought it would be nice if, for once, she could be the parent who got a smile or even a hug in return for some sugary cereal. It would be nice to receive an easy-to-get smile from Max before she no longer had that opportunity, because a smile from her son was still a smile from her son, even if it was also sugar for an eight-year-old boy from the parent that knew better.

She moved on, leaving the Coco Pops on the shelf. It was lazy parenting, but she would have treated the children now and again if she didn't think Laurence had done that enough for the both of them.

But it was more than just Coco Pops vs. Rice Krispies. Inside the disagreement was resentment she hadn't aired before because one half of a couple can shape the other half. She had to balance the overgenerosity that made her the ungenerous half, the half that said 'no', the half that insisted on Alice coming home early, or Max doing his homework before screentime.

She imagined the conversation at home.

Laurence: 'Shall we see if Mummy will buy some Coco Pops?'

Max: 'I bet she won't, Dad. She never does.'

Laurence: 'Yeah, but come on, kiddo, it's worth a try. Don't ask, don't get.'

A year ago she'd been shopping with Max in tow and spotted a Nintendo box in the trolley hidden under salad leaves and bags of fruit. She deduced that Max had planted it there, picked up from the electronics aisle in the hope it might go through the checkout, unnoticed. Lisa passed it over to the checkout man. 'I don't think we need this.' The next week Laurence did the weekly shop with Max and they came back with a Nintendo.

Once upon a time, a highly evolved female ape-descendant had a son on a planet that orbited one of the billions of stars in a galaxy called the Milky Way. That society of ape-descendants made computers, some of which were for work and some for play. And the son wanted one for play but the female said 'no'. They argued and argued, but her son got a play-computer anyway. Two years later, cracks in the universe appeared. A rug was pulled from under the female's feet, revealing nothing below.

Chapter 22

When Lisa got back from the supermarket she saw lights on in her daughter's room and downstairs in the living room. She opened the front door with a bag in each hand and called into the house. Max appeared from the kitchen. 'Dad's gone for a run and Alice is upstairs in her room. She's probably listening to music so she won't come down. I'll help you, Mummy.'

He went to the car and came back with the rest of the shopping, nearly his own bodyweight bulging in the bags, clearly satisfied to show off his strength. He lifted the bags onto the table one by one and went about his scan, taking each item out the bag and placing them in his own value system, a patchwork of rules mostly dependent on salt and sugar content. At least that's how Lisa thought it went. Slowly, the shopping spread out over the kitchen table on top of his homework. Lisa watched for the moment he found the Coco Pops, because in the supermarket she had changed her mind and bought some, and she didn't want to miss that smile.

She started putting away the things he'd taken out as if the two of them were working on a production line, just that Max didn't know and it became a little dance that happened without arrangement.

'Have you done your homework?'

'I was about to do it, but you wanted me to help with the bags!'

'Why don't you set yourself up with your work and I'll bring you some toast? Butter and marmite?'

'Yes, okay.'

'Yes, okay. *Thank you, Mummy*?'

'Thanks, Mum.'

Good enough. She moved the shopping to the counter and Max took out his work. As she put the shopping away in the fridge and cupboards, she asked as casually as she could, 'Do you think your sister has been a bit angry recently?'

*

To Max, there was something exciting about being asked this question but he wasn't sure what it was. Perhaps it was being asked about his sister when she wasn't in the room. 'I don't know,' he said. 'I don't think so.'

'Or maybe a bit sad?'

He turned and faced his mother and said quietly, 'I saw her crying last week.'

'When?'

'In her room, I could hear her on the phone, so I looked in and saw her crying.'

'Who was she speaking to?'

'I don't know.'

*

Did everyone but her in the family know that Alice was miserable? Lisa boiled the kettle and armed herself with tea, then left Max to his work.

The stairs made familiar creaks and groans as she climbed them. A few paces away from the top was her daughter's bedroom door, which was closed. Lisa slipped a finger through the handles of both mugs so that they were balanced together in one hand, and knocked gently with the other. Her daughter didn't respond, so she opened the door slowly, holding the white flag of ceasefire, or surrender.

Alice had headphones on and the music was loud enough for Lisa to hear it, although not distinctly. She was working at her desk with her back to the door.

'Alice?' she said loudly, and her daughter's glance flicked up to the mirror in front of her, but she didn't turn around, so her back remained facing her mother. Lisa didn't tell her daughter to turn down the music, but it did occur to her.

If her daughter's hard eyes were a gun, trigger pulled, then this evening's eyes were those with a finger on the trigger and Lisa was reminded that the last time they had spoken Alice had called her a spiteful bitch.

'Thank you,' Alice said, turning around and putting a Post-it note down as a coaster on her bedside table.

'What are you listening to?'

Alice shook her head, 'You haven't heard of them.'

Swirling in the room, just behind the air and oxygen were the questions the mother had for her daughter. Questions that were measuring tools for their relationship, on which other questions might be asked, if they could be. But she was still a little way from asking them, so for now smaller questions would suffice. Alice didn't say anything else, so Lisa had another go: 'What are you working on?'

'Schoolwork.'

Lisa pointed at the bed. 'Can I sit?'

'Your house, your rules, Lisa.'

She looked at her daughter and saw the repetitions of herself and her husband and the evolution away from them too. Alice had been a thing that began in her womb and then she got too big so she was born and every step since then – sometimes with her mother's help but now exclusively on her own – she was establishing herself in her own right as entirely her own person. And yet she was still a child.

'Max said that you were crying the other night, and I would have let that pass, but your aunt also said that I should ask you if everything was okay. She didn't tell me what it was about, but she said I should ask.'

'Looks like you've done your homework. Max? Aunt Chloe? How was the annual catchup with your sister? Or did you bump into her?'

'I don't think that's fair, Alice.'

'And what about Dad? Spoken to him recently? Stupid question – of course you haven't.'

'Can you explain to me why you're angry?'

'And what about Sara, who I speak to more often than you do?'

'I saw Sara today, as it happens.'

Alice stood up and lifted the chair she was sitting on, placing it so that they were face to face and not far apart, distorting an intimacy which she used for scorn. She leaned forward with her elbows on her knees. 'Seeing as you're so interested in my life, do you know that my boyfriend dumped me? I asked him why and do you know what he said about me? He said I was distant and cold and I thought, I wonder where I got that from? He said I was a closed book. So, I thought to myself, which of my role models spends too much time at work and not enough time with her husband? I don't want to be like you, Mum. I don't want to be stressed about material things that don't matter to me. I want to be able to show affection to those around me. I'm tired of being the emotional surrogate for Max and Dad, and Chloe and Sara. So, if you don't mind, I'm going back to my schoolwork, and I'd appreciate it if you left me alone.'

Lisa's emotions sprinted ahead of her and ran towards someone in particular and it surprised her that the person was Laurence, the support in her marriage. With the stun of adrenaline, it was Laurence she wanted in the room with her, so that they could talk to their daughter together and on the one hand, that was perfectly normal to her and on the other, it was becoming perfectly alien. She stood up and left while Alice's words had not yet landed, still falling, but gathering speed.

*

It was about time someone told her mother the truth, held up a mirror and gave Lisa a taste of her own medicine. Be distant, Alice told herself, and strong enough to push her mother away. She wasn't going to open up about the break-up to her on-off mother, she didn't want to shed one more tear on some boy.

The dawning truth of her parents' marriage had revealed itself when she'd skipped school one day. Alice had been suspicious when she and her father had sat down to talk about the woman she'd seen leaving their house. She was meant to be at school but had skipped it as she had two free periods in a row and the teacher for her only class was off sick. Her father dismissed her questions so casually that it convinced her: the woman was another architect working on a project with him. It had been a business meeting. Then she pushed him, asked if he was cheating on her mother, which was when he got angry, accused her of being a child who had no idea what she was talking about. Then at the bus stop, he had come clean with the truth and Alice felt so sorry for her father because her mother had asked for an open marriage, and suggested that they see other people when her father had wanted to work it out.

She took out her phone and texted her aunt Chloe: *I've had a big argument with your sister.*

*

Lisa stood outside her daughter's room in shock, her daughter's words still being processed like bullets that needed interpreting before they could pierce their target. She forced herself to see Alice as the teenager that she was and repress the anger at her child.

She felt the weight in her feet shift as she walked down the stairs, letting her daughter be, but halfway down she turned around, walked back up the stairs and opened the door to her daughter's room. Alice was back at her desk, although she was clearly not working and likely shaken up by adrenaline too. She looked surprised to see her mother.

Lisa said, 'You're an intelligent person, Alice, but not so much that you know everything there is to know... yet. You don't know about boundaries, that they're there to protect yourself. Mothers don't raise them up against their daughters, but they might do for their sisters. I love your aunt, actually very much, but it's not for you to get involved between us. Stop trying to fix everyone around you. You can't.' She folded her arms, and if she hadn't been so caught up in the moment, would have realised she was leaning forward, her head tilted into a stance similar to the one her daughter adopted for hard eyes.

'And you should never let anyone tell you that you are distant, if it's in their interest to knock you down. It seems to me like this boyfriend of yours, who you never introduced me to or even mentioned to me, is knocking your confidence on purpose. He probably thinks you're too good for him and the only way he can keep himself level with you, is to belittle you. You don't see that, so you blame yourself, then me because that's so much easier to do. I doubt this boy is any good for you, or indeed, good for anyone, himself included.

'So if it's easier to pick on me than realise that your ex-boyfriend is a shit, so be it. That's what I'm here for. That's what all mothers are here for, to be the perennial punchbag. For as long as we're here, that is. Because I won't be around forever. But see how far that gets you, picking on the people that love you. Just because I'm an easy target, doesn't mean I deserve to be a target.'

She stepped back behind the doorframe, reached for the handle and closed the door quietly. Then she went down the stairs calmly one step at a time and went through what had just happened. No, she hadn't raised her voice, which was good. And yes, she felt that what she'd said was fair and right, which was also good and no, she didn't want to see her daughter right now.

She went into the living room to be alone and felt the pulse of her heart in her chest. She took out her phone. It shook in her hand and she felt the blood pumping in the tip of her finger as she scrolled to find her mother's phone number.

'Would you mind coming round to pick up the children?'

'Of course. Do they need to stay the night here?'

'If you wouldn't mind, and can you feed them too? I've just given Max a snack. It will mean Dad will have to do the school run tomorrow.'

'No problem. I'll send him round now.'

'I need a night in with Laurence.'

'I know, darling. I know. I think it's time you told him and I know he'll be there for you in ways you didn't even realise you needed.'

'Thanks, Mum. See Dad in forty-five mins or so.'

'Bye, darling.'

In the silent living room, things fell into place ahead of her like slabs of pavement leading the way. She wasn't angry or sad, not scared or complacent. She was just herself in her home, and there were things in front of her now.

Which one gaslighted her husband; which one never spoke to her sister; which one got angry at her friend's support; and which one deserved her lot? Her daughter had thrown a lot at her feet. Lisa could feel herself accepting the blame her daughter had cast upon her, and her urge to reach out and find support grew.

She went back to the kitchen and helped her son with his homework. Not long after, the key turned in the front door and Laurence appeared. He ruffled his son's hair and asked about his homework. Lisa smiled at him and stood up. Even though he was sweating through his shirt, she put the palm of her hand on his chest and kissed him.

'You're running more than usual. Is it every day?' she asked.

'Yeah, I guess so. I'm not really trying to, but I do want to get into a routine.'

'My father's coming round to pick the kids up. I thought we could have a night to ourselves.'

She looked for his reaction and at first he seemed cool with the approach, then mischief in his eyes spread across his face. 'I could put a bottle of wine in the fridge?'

'I already have,' she said. 'Max, can you go and pack your bag, please?'

'Can I take my Nintendo?'

'Have you finished your homework?'

'Yes.'

'Then, yes.'

As Max ran upstairs she asked Laurence to tell Alice to pack a bag too. 'I can't speak to her right now.'

She started preparing things in the kitchen for a different supper for herself and Laurence. Sometime later, a knock came from the front door and Lisa heard the arrhythmic thud of two steps taken at the same time as Alice came down the stairs to open the door to her grandfather.

Chapter 23

'Hi, Grandpa,' Alice said. She swung her arms around his neck. 'This is a fun surprise.'

They walked into the kitchen where Lisa was and the first thing he said was, 'How are you, darling?' in a tone that caught Alice's attention immediately. He made an earnest face at Alice and asked, 'Are you being good to your mother?'

Her eyes darted between her mother and grandfather. Had her mother recruited her own father as some sort of sympathy tool? She wouldn't, but Alice was caught between judgement of her mother and love for her grandfather. She was confused and so was her answer. 'I try, Grandpa. Sometimes it's harder than you'd think.'

He looked at her with a gruff quality she had never seen before and said, 'Right now, I would appreciate it if you could be there for your mother.' Alice glared at her mother, who didn't look back at her. Her mother, who was manipulating more of her family; her mother, who had no moral leg to stand on. Alice didn't know what her grandfather meant exactly, but it was stark that they were talking about her mother while she was in the room – her mother at the centre of everything, her mother at the table.

New emotions were painting the image she kept of her grandfather. This paternal protectiveness was novel. She'd never seen her grandfather act as a father. It felt like sternness to the point of admonishment, like there was something she was to blame for.

'Right.' He moved on. 'Can you go upstairs and ask your father to come and say hello, please?'

'Dad?' began Lisa.

'I just want to say hello, that's all. He *is* my son-in-law.' Then to his granddaughter, 'I'll see you in the car.'

Alice wondered what was happening around her and watched her mother who went back to cooking and looking in the fridge, trying to look anywhere but at her daughter. It was just the two of them in the kitchen and her mother was hiding from her because it was clear that Lisa had used her own father to manipulate her daughter. Alice wanted to take Max aside and explain that their mother was manipulative, that she had driven away her husband and was breaking up their family, and she wanted to do this in front of her mother who was ignoring her.

She didn't want to go to her mother's parents' house, but neither did she want to stay at home. What Alice wanted was for her mother to stop ignoring her. 'You know,' she waited for her mother to look at her, 'I don't blame Dad.' She waited for a reaction then walked out when she didn't get one, coming back down a moment later carrying her and her brother's bags, with Max and Laurence following behind.

In the back of her grandfather's car, Alice reached over her little brother to help him with his seatbelt. 'I can do it myself,' he said. But she wasn't listening to him, she was listening to Grandpa and her father on the pavement.

'Very kind of you, Dan. I can't remember the last time we had a night in to ourselves.'

'Our pleasure. I know Lisa has got a huge amount on her mind, so it's important for you to be there for each other. She needs you, Laurence.'

Alice strained to see her father's face in the dark, but he was turned away from the light coming from their family home so it was hidden in shadow. 'Yes, with everything going on at work and the kids, she's got a lot on her plate,' said Laurence but it sounded like he was feeling out the right answer. 'Thanks again.' Then he tapped on the roof of the car and walked back to the house.

Alice watched her father walk back up the dark street and garden to her home lit with lights shining through the windows. She'd forgotten to turn off the light in her room. She wondered what conversations lay ahead between her mother and father, if this was the beginning of the end of her family, and all of a sudden, she felt bad for her mother.

Her grandfather started the engine. 'What's for dinner, Gramps?' she asked.

*

As they ate dinner, everything in the kitchen was very still and yet acute to Lisa's senses. The tick of the clock was deep in her ears, the glare of the ceiling lights burned the back of her eyes. The walls surrounded them, stalking their conversation, crouched and ready to pounce. Lisa finished the last bite on her plate and closed knife and fork together. Laurence helped himself to more food from the dish between them, and she watched him eat.

She had the constant feeling that she was about to catch something move out the corner of her eye, but every time she glanced she saw nothing. Dinner didn't feel familiar, it felt like two separate lives coming together to discuss the bits that overlapped, exposed by the lack of children.

Laurence was perfunctory and investigative in his conversation. He had asked half a dozen times if she was okay, and what was up and was there anything she wanted to talk about and could she let him know if there was anything he could do. But at no point did he admit that her father had mentioned something, as she knew her father would have.

She guessed at the twists and turns going on in Laurence's head. On the one hand, it was very simple: 'Darling, your father said that something was up. He never does this, so it sounded serious.' And on the other: 'Shall we talk about our marriage?' Or maybe, 'I need to come clean.'

This was the real conversation played out over dinner: the unspoken conversation which swam under the surface next to the spoken one, never breaching. Laurence played concern, but not so well as he outed himself, his concern limited by his own culpability for letting their marriage sink to the sea bed. Yet still Lisa wanted him to be there for her and in some ways *needed* him to be there for her. She was waiting for him to step up and be the partner she hoped for, the partner she knew he could be and the partner that he had been, but only if he could come close to her and explain why he was distant with her. If that meant admitting he was having an affair, if he could just scrape that honesty together, she might forgive him and she could tell him she had cancer and they could support each other.

Of course, she could always be wrong about the affair. How would he react if she was wrong? How hurt would he be when he found out she'd held it against him all the while she was dealing with cancer on her own? While they were at home without the kids, it was the perfect opportunity to tell him about the results.

She decided that in fact, these things didn't matter. It was his complete and total withdrawal of intimacy from their marriage that mattered. What else could that be other than an affair? She thought about this while they talked and it all seemed too bizarre and too obvious. Finally he finished his own plate and said, 'Your father seemed to think you were stressed. Is everything okay? I know work is up in the air at the moment.'

Work was always up in the air. Her work lived in the air because he brought up her career more than she brought up his and now, it meant something else – it was his excuse, his lie, so that they could talk about anything else other than their marriage.

'Are you having an affair?' she asked. In that moment, the thing in the corner of her eye vanished, and the glare in her eyes and the ticking of the clock in her ears went away, and the walls took a step back. The whites of his eyes grew brighter and his ears turned red.

'I could ask you the same thing,' he said.

What the fuck? 'Are you really asking me that?'

She had an image of both her and Laurence sitting on the sofa on Thursday night, looking up at the ceiling. She imagined her husband with a faceless woman pulling the old sheets from the mattress, then holding up and spreading smooth a new one, catching each other's eye and sharing a smile stolen from her own marriage.

She watched each of his actions like they were a rehearsal, a stream of cues: cutlery dropped to plate, back straightened, jaw dropped, head flopped to the side.

'What's brought this on?' *This question is on you*. 'No,' he answered when she didn't, 'I'm not having an affair. Is that what's upsetting you? Did you tell your father you think I'm having an affair? Lisa, how could you keep that buried?' *Accusation*. 'I can't believe you'd speak to your father about this before speaking to me.' *Blame*. 'So, let me start – you're the one who's been distant.' *Divert and shame*. 'I haven't been able to talk to you, and yes, that means I've been distant too, so, we're both to blame.' *But you started it*.

She heard her daughter's voice saying, 'He said I was cold. I wonder where I got that from?'

He continued and she listened. 'Look: this is normal for parents with young children. We're focusing on the parenting at the cost of the marriage, but it's nothing we can't work out. I'm here for you now and I want to know what's going on. We're here for each other and the children. It's you and me, we can work anything out.' He reached out and his hand rested on hers.

Her hand turned under his so that their fingers interlocked and they sat in the space of the kitchen holding each other's hands, like they did in bed each night, before they went to sleep.

'From my end, I promise it will be better and I'll be more present,' he said. 'I'll try harder and things will get better, I know they will. And I'm sorry, I hadn't realised how this was affecting you.'

She said nothing, so he continued. 'Please, tell me what's wrong.' She felt lonely, sitting at the table holding her husband's hand. Lonely because she felt foolish. She finished the wine in her glass and looked down at the table. Their hands were still interlocked, her other hand balancing a fork with her index finger. 'You know, you always do that with the fork, when you're thinking,' he said. She put the fork down.

'Work is up in the air,' she said. 'I think they're finally going to push me out. Jack doesn't have my back anymore and I'm being forced to take pitches with Adam, because they need to lock down my clients before firing me.'

'Of all the people in the office: *him*?'

Fighting his way out of the corner, he stirred. Now Laurence was animated and started suggesting things: like misogyny or office politics and things she should do, like negotiating or meeting them halfway, or looking for a new job, or soliciting an employment lawyer.

Laurence filled her wine glass again and she wondered, if alcohol killed brain cells, could it also kill cancerous brain cells? And if it did, maybe she could drink hard liquor and cure herself.

'How was your conversation with Mr Carter?' she asked.

Laurence shrugged. 'Max is going through a tough time at school. I think Mr Carter's right, he's gone quiet. I asked him about it in the car later and he just looked out of the window. He's a sensitive little boy.'

Lisa picked up her fork again, between her fingertip and the table. 'I think it'd help Max to talk about it with his dad. He'll open up eventually. Why don't you spend a morning or afternoon with him this weekend?'

'I already told him what I think. I said if anyone's bullying him, he should punch them in the face.'

Lisa felt the space her body occupied as if she was being touched all over her skin. She tried not to move or change the movements she was already making, like playing with the fork she hadn't realised she was playing with. Like being aware of a gaze, his gaze, and not showing that awareness because she knew Laurence was looking for a reaction. She tried not to sit up, tried not move her legs, but something doubtlessly gave her away, some little twitch she was unaware of.

'Which I can see you think was a bad idea,' he said.

'Not at all! I think he needs to hear something like that, but perhaps in context. Like self-defence?'

Laurence took his hand away from hers and leaned back on his chair with his arms up and fingers interlocked behind his head. 'I said if someone's bullying him and no teacher has done anything about it, he should take matters into his own hands. Life's too short to be bullied.'

'Yes, life is too short,' she said. 'Blink, and it'll be over.'

She felt the familiar rush through her cheeks and into her eyes, just as she had in the counselling room earlier that day. 'Alice is still angry with me,' she said. 'I tried to speak to her, but... Nothing.' *I don't blame Dad.*

Laurence stood up and started clearing the table, a thing to do to keep his eyes away from hers and not the thing you did at the end of a meal because it needed to be done. 'At her age everything's transient,' he said. 'I wouldn't worry. She'll move on, whatever it is. Maybe I'll have a word with her.'

He was claiming her distance from Alice as his closeness, but Lisa couldn't put this into words. How could he be so sure about their daughter?

'Alice is worried about us. She told me on Friday night. She said that it was obvious you weren't happy.'

'Did she give any reason?' he said with this back to her as he continued the washing-up. 'We don't argue. We function pretty well.'

What Lisa wanted to say was that Alice saw it wasn't the words they used, but the words they didn't. But she was done with distance, done trying to call it out. Now, she wanted intimacy. She stood up, took the dishcloth from him and dried his hands. 'We can do this later,' she said, took his arm and slipped it around her waist and there was willingness between them.

Chapter 24

The sooner Lisa could forget the first time she had sex, the better. Mostly because it hadn't been what she'd expected and the stark intimacy, in such quantity and in a new, physical form, was overwhelming to her at fifteen.

If she could go back in time, and if the imagination of the forty-something self could pick and choose how the event unfolded for her teenage self, how would she reconstruct the experience? At first, she thought she'd change a lot. For starters, how it felt, and the *Star Wars* duvet cover on the boy's bed. Maybe even change the partner altogether.

She and the boy were in the same class at school and there were rumours that they liked each other before she was even aware of liking the boy herself. So, one day they started kissing. They spent more time with each other, kissing and taking every opportunity to get a little more physical until one afternoon his parents were away at the right time. There had also been some talking and some getting to know each other but now, thirty years later, it was the kissing she remembered. He was a good kisser and she liked kissing him and on reflection she realised that she probably wouldn't change a thing. Neither of them really knew what they were doing and that was good. It was discovery, no hint of instruction. Now she thought about it, she'd even keep the duvet because it was the flag that claimed the memory as one of innocence. Although she would like to have waited a little longer before losing her virginity, maybe one or even two more years. Alice's age. Oh god. Lisa supposed that this boyfriend of her daughter's might have been her first love and how terrible it would have been for her to have had this first – hopefully not formative – experience.

Laurence started to snore. Of course he would, as he'd had sex and half a bottle of wine and he operated like clockwork. Lisa couldn't fathom how some people could be so unaware of themselves.

She turned away from him and, as if counting sheep, she began recalling each partner she'd had in her life. Some had been entirely forgotten and she remembered them only now with effort, and others had been purposefully forgotten. But awake and adrift in the darkness next to her husband, they too came out of the woodwork.

She traced a line like a thread through stitches, from the first with the *Star Wars* bedsheets to the one sleeping next to her, keeping her awake.

She sat up, rustling the duvet as loudly as possible. After all the things she'd been through in the last five days, it wasn't fair that her sleep should be taken from her too. She tutted, but all that happened was the snoring got louder.

'Laurence?'

Still nothing, so she turned the hypersomniac on his side and although he gave a few involuntary twitches and grunts, he didn't actually wake. The snoring stopped, replaced with busy, satisfied breathing, which was more irritating.

She wondered where that boy was now – the one whose virginities they took from each other – and what had taken him there. Was he still alive? Was he healthy? She thought about the past lovers she was close to, and the ones that fell into the mistake bracket. She thought about the ones she had pushed away, and the ones who had withdrawn from her.

A beam of moonlight disappeared as the moon floated behind a cloud and even the shadows and shapes disappeared in the pitch black. In the darkness, Lisa's consciousness blended into the night, filling the room so that she wasn't sure where her thoughts ended and her body began.

In this ether of sleeplessness, she heard her daughter's voice again: *I don't blame Dad*. What was going on in her daughter's world? she wondered. The exclusion was torture, especially now.

Out of the ether came more voices, those of her old boyfriends and past lovers. They filled the room. Lisa found herself talking to her old partners, asking them about their lives and in turn they asked about hers. Each one asked about her children, and she replied that she was worried about them.

She was worried about Max, and not being there for him. How not having his mother might change the person he would become. She was worried he still needed so much more nurturing before he found his feet.

But mostly, she was worried for Alice, who was intelligent and funny and lovely, but also fierce and angry and unhappy. She was worried how much more angry she might become if she lost her mother.

In the room so dark she didn't know if her eyes were open or closed, the voices took form in hallucinations, becoming faces, looming in the room which was now an extension of her mind. They stood over her and spoke in unison. She didn't want to listen to them but they got louder and louder until she was compelled to take notice. 'Tell your daughter that you're ill', her past lovers said, 'even if you don't tell your husband. Your daughter wants to be treated like an adult.' Lisa sat up in bed. This hadn't occurred to her and she thought it was a good idea.

Chapter 25

That night, before Lisa thought about her past lovers and before she turned her husband to his side, she made love to him for the last time.

When they went to bed, they did so in each other's arms but with their own, very different reasons for doing so. For Laurence, it can't have been a surprise to be making love to his wife, although perhaps it was a relief, because there had been tension building between them. However, mostly, it felt like he followed the relief because it aligned with his impulses.

For her, she was reaching out and grasping for the connection she desperately missed, at the time in her life she needed it most. A gesture of creation to bring life to their marriage, and the support and love she sought. She went to bed with him hoping for connection, but already this hope was hollowed out by doubt. As they took off each other's clothes and fell into bed, she let go that he would never meet her expectations. She let go of the distance between them and her doubts in him, but not entirely.

In the very back of her mind – the unpresent part that verged on subconscious – Lisa was piecing together why she was alone: she was hoping for connection from a person who wouldn't give it. In a way, the affair didn't matter. Her husband was the source of her loneliness and he was a foot placed on a loose rock giving way.

The reason she had sex that night wasn't to see if they could reconnect. It was to witness that if he was cheating on her, how deep his deceit would go. And if he wasn't cheating on her, for her to witness how shallow he was, by having sex without confronting their distance.

And while they made love she felt detached from her body in the bedroom lit between the light from the bathroom and the gloom from the window.

A seed of rejection was planted that night and the kernel of the seed was strength and independence that would ensure, if she only had months left, she would not be alone.

In time, she would look back on this night and realise that Laurence never had a chance. No way would he have seen things her way and done what she needed him to do, but it was as good a way as any to say goodbye to her husband.

Chapter 26

The next morning Lisa was at ease with life in a way she hadn't been in a long while. Was it possible that it was the release of tension from the night before, she wondered, before she realised it was something else – no children. She waited for Laurence to wake up and when he did, he mirrored her smile as he came to the same realisation – no children!

They got up slowly, lying in bed, chatting about what they didn't have to do that morning, which was usually wake up Alice three times and hold a long negotiation with Max to change out of his pyjamas. No kids' breakfast, packed lunch, school run, traffic, chat with other parents, forgotten judo kit, requests for pocket money or advances on pocket money. 'I could get used to this,' he said.

They had showers, him first then her, and helped choose each other's the clothes for the day. It was ideal, but Lisa was well aware that now it was an ideal fiction. When she came downstairs, Laurence had cleared dinner and had the beginnings of breakfast on the table.

'I was going to ask if you wanted eggs and bacon or fruit and yoghurt, but then I couldn't think of a reason not to have both.' It was a nice sentiment to be greeted with and she felt appreciated.

They sat down and started eating. Everything in the kitchen was calm and she remembered what normal adult life was like, but eventually the crack in the glass appeared, Laurence's small talk. 'So,' he said, 'what are you going to do about Adam at work? If you want, I can introduce you to a lawyer. I know several employment specialists.'

'Sure,' Lisa said, trying to tread the fine line between satiating her husband's ego and keeping herself sane, while he explained the solutions to her problems, without invitation.

'For what it's worth, I've been thinking you should look into constructive dismissal and get a new job. I bet there are competitors out there that would want to poach you. Maybe one in London that pays what you deserve.'

'Good idea,' she said.

'And if you come to the table with a job offer in hand or an injunction for wrongful dismissal, then I'm sure they'll sit up and make you a better offer to stay. They might even make you Chief Exec.'

'Generally, people don't initiate legal proceedings to get to Chief Executive.'

'Hm. Good point. Or you could set up on your own, as a consultant.'

'I'm going to speak to Chloe for legal advice.'

'Chloe? Really? I thought she stopped practising law.'

'She was a very good lawyer in her day, before she decided that the meaning of life wasn't a regular pay cheque.'

'Well, money's important. And I don't like the way she says my name.'

'That's just her sign of affection!'

'It is not out of affection, as well you know. It's the tone she says it: *La-Ree.*'

It was amusing to see this unearthed past grievance as a still-very-alive chip on his shoulder. After Chloe met

Laurence the first time, she had asked Lisa questions which weren't so much about seeking answers as expressing her opinions: 'And you *do* love him? Do you think he's particularly cerebral? Don't you find his humour a little irritating?' The annoying thing was that Lisa's answers to these questions had been genuine: yes, she found him intelligent; no, she liked his sense of humour; and yes, in time, she could see herself in love with him. But these answers, when she'd given them to Chloe, sounded like ungenuine ripostes to her sister's concerns.

Laurence put down a pot of coffee. Lisa could smell the beans that he'd just ground and the milk he had warmed on the stove – a morning ceremony that was allowed to flourish when time permitted. Nothing was hurried that morning and there was no noise of four individuals trying to make their own version of breakfast.

The current family impasse was what should happen to the oats. Laurence liked porridge, whereas Alice preferred overnight oats with apple grated on top. Then there was Team Toast made up of mother and son, itself divided between white bread (Max) and brown sourdough (Lisa). Today, there was no never-ending mission to get them to eat enough food (Alice) or the right sort of food (Max).

At the end of breakfast, Laurence cleared the table. He got his coat and rucksack and they both went to the front door.

'Let me know how your day goes,' he said. 'Don't let those fuckers get you down.' He kissed her on the cheek, then closed the front door, with its familiar clink-clang and the rusty screech of the garden gate after that.

Lisa went back to the kitchen table and texted her sister: *Cancel everything. Lunch please, on me.*

Like pieces of Lego the size of mountains falling into place, Lisa felt that a new world was being constructed.

Tectonic plates were shifting beneath her feet, building a new path and revealing a world where everything looked different.

Chapter 27

When Granny wasn't looking, that's when Max struck. He hopped off the old wooden stool that seemed as old as she was, then climbed back on it, this time with his feet on the seat to reach the cupboard. Inside, the multipack of Mini Cheddars waited for his greedy little fingers.

Max took one out expertly, like the Artful Dodger he'd read about in a book, without crunching the plastic wrapper – he knew how to do this – and slipped it silently into his pocket. The Assassin of Lunchtime Snacks. All this happened behind Granny's back in a split second. Then he popped down so that he was back sitting on the stool again when she turned around and smiled at him. She handed him his packed lunch which contained only one packet of Mini Cheddars. 'Thank you, Granny,' he said, stifling his hammering pulse, gripped by the thrill of crime.

Then for a second he was a rabbit in headlights caught out by the silent one, his sister in the doorway. He was as still as winter until Alice gave him a smile, and he knew he was in the clear. He smiled back and let his shoulders drop. One packet in his lunch box and one in his pocket!

'Hello, darling,' said Granny, when she saw Alice. 'Do you take a packed lunch?'

Alice smiled at her grandmother who didn't know a child's lunch from a teenager's. 'There's a canteen at my school.'

'Is the food any good? I heard school food isn't good anymore.'

'I have my allowance so I can nip to the shop and buy something if there's nothing I want to eat. That said, a top-up would always be welcome.'

'Help yourself to a fiver from my purse, but don't tell your mother and don't spend it on fast food.'

Alice smiled. 'I eat healthily, Granny. Better than Max does. For instance, he's got a second packet of Mini Cheddars in his pocket.' From behind their grandmother's back Max raised a middle finger at his sister.

'Yes, I know he does,' said Granny. 'I wasn't born yesterday.' Max nearly fell off his stool. 'Next time, ask me and of course I'll give you another packet. Now,' said their grandmother, 'are both of you looking after your mother?'

The grandchildren looked at each other, Team Grandchildren, trying to figure out what was the right answer. 'I helped her with the shopping last night,' said Max.

'I think Mum's okay for the moment,' said Alice. 'I think she gets a lot of sympathy from everyone else around her.'

'Is that what you think?' said Cath. 'Let me tell you, there are very adult things happening in your mother's life which she will discuss with you when she can, but she will need your love and support.'

'I think you're entitled to your opinion, Granny.'

'What did you say?'

'Let's just say there are two sides to any story,' said Alice. Max glanced between Alice and their grandmother.

'I think you don't know what you're talking about, young girl. So, I'll repeat the point: my daughter – your mother – needs all the love and support you can provide right now and I'd be grateful if you provided that.'

*

Being ticked off by her grandmother had a powerful effect on Alice because it was so rare. Then she checked the guilt. Of course her grandparents would take their daughter's side when her marriage was falling apart. What Alice wanted to say to her grandmother was, 'You don't know anything', 'Has she got you around her little finger too?', and 'If you knew what I knew'. But she didn't dare, not in front of this version of her grandmother.

Her grandfather came into the room, gave his wife a kiss and they held hands, and her grandmother smiled at Alice as if they had never had a disagreement in their lives, let alone a moment ago. So what if the affair was her mother's doing? So what if she was having an affair too? Lisa would be upset that her marriage was ending and Alice knew then that it would soon be time to stop judging her.

Chapter 28

Lisa thought she was in for a relatively quiet morning at the office before lunch with Chloe, and nothing more. Little more to do than smooth things over with Jack. There were no signs of drama as her colleagues milled around, nothing out of the ordinary in the way they greeted her and no din between rows of desks or around the water fountain.

But then she opened her email on her desktop. Nearly a dozen had arrived from Jack, from his personal account, and she realised she'd not replied or contacted him once in the past twenty-four hours. His last email simply said: *Don't say I didn't try. Too late now.*

So much had happened that she'd forgotten she was in the middle of a boardroom civil war. Seeing his emails now – and the helplessness in them – her disappointment in him gave way to the value of their friendship and history together. She began to write a response but decided on a tête-à-tête after typing the first line. When she got to his office on the penultimate floor, he was nowhere to be seen. Not only that, his office was empty of the few personal effects he kept there.

'Pam, have you seen Jack?'

Pam looked nervous, which irritated Lisa. 'Pam?'

'I don't know what I'm supposed to say. Jack doesn't

work here anymore?' Pam could not hold eye contact with Lisa.

'You're joking! He was Chief Executive yesterday. Only the exec committee or the board can fire him, and I sit on the former.'

'The committee and the board met yesterday. I think that's why he was trying to get in touch. Your vote was discounted in your absence. I took the minutes.'

'Fucking hell! Who did this to him?'

'Adam led the motion. It was very sad. I had to clear his desk for him because he stormed out of the building. They cut off his emails at midnight.'

'Brutal. Who's the interim CEO?'

'Adam, again.'

'Oh, fuck, Pam! This is a disaster. Why didn't you call me immediately?'

Pam looked panicked.

'It's okay, Pam. It's not your job to keep me abreast of things when I've been absent.'

'I think you should go and see Adam,' she said. 'He'll be expecting it, I'm sure. He's in his office on the fourth floor.'

Lisa glanced at her watch. 'I'm sure he'll come find me at some point today.' She gave Pam a well-meaning smile and left.

Back in her own office, she called Jack, but his phone went to voicemail and she realised that it too would have been cut off upon his dismissal, so she called his personal number. 'Lisa,' he said down the line.

'Hi, Jack. I just heard the news. What's going on?'

'You mean, what's gone on? I tried to speak to you yesterday and all weekend but you didn't answer me. This might have been avoided, if you had been there at the executive committee meeting.'

'Let's not begin blamefully,' she said, managing him. 'You, for one, have had a campaign to get me working with Adam and that's clearly backfired. So, tell me what happened and we can go from there.'

'Are you out of your fucking mind? I have been balancing the other executives to keep my job and yours! They've wanted to carve up the department we built – *you and I built* – and integrate it into the rest of the company. The department, I might add, that *you* lead and poured your blood, sweat and tears into. I'll fucking kill them. I'm speaking to lawyers. I'm going to fight this.'

'Jack,' Lisa said calmly, 'tell me how it happened.'

He filled her in: Adam had been canvassing the executive committee to remove Lisa, take her clients and pay her off if necessary. Too much of the company's business came from her, her department was too large and there was the risk that she might leave for a competitor. Because she had shown an unwillingness to work with Adam, the other executives backed him to restructure the company, remove Jack and manage Lisa out. She would be next. 'Don't let them, Lisa. Don't let them take away what you've built. I'm in contact with a couple of the old guard on the board, but they were outvoted. If you can get to them, maybe you can stop Adam.'

It was hard to guage if Jack was offering to help for her sake, or if this was his best way to get back into the company, and she was a means to that end. 'Jack, I'm sick. That's the personal matter HR told you about. It's a tumour in my brain, likely cancer. So I'm not sure I'm the right person to mount a defence on your behalf. I'm not sure if I'll even be *able* to take your job even if the board voted for me.'

'Lisa, I'm so sorry.'

But her mind was not focused on sympathy for herself. She was thinking that if she was about to be dismissed, a payout could be attractive while she focused on her home and health. That said, speaking with Jack had stirred something in her, a sense of righteousness that her career, which had taken so much of her life to build, should not be surrendered. Her resolved toughened and she tried to figure out what she needed to do.

'You must be livid,' she said. 'But I bet they paid you off well.'

'He betrayed me!' That was odd, Lisa thought. Why would Adam have betrayed Jack?

'But Lisa, who cares? Next to our health, this is all meaningless. They've taken everything I've done in the last three decades away from me and they did it in a day.' Then he shouted, 'It was Kristallnacht, damn it!'

'Everything *we've* done, Jack.'

Lisa stared out the window with her hand up for shade, Jack's frustration being so much less than the glare from the sun, so much less than the other things in her life. She stared through another office window across the street, at another employee of another company talking on their own phone. Looking down the road at rows of office buildings in both directions, she thought of the people working inside. And there was Jack, miles away, shouting into a phone he was holding in his hand. Shouting at the means to an end that had become an end in itself. Who could blame him for caring so much, given how much of his life he'd poured into his career.

Lisa realised that she didn't care anymore.

There was relief in work too, in that she hadn't thought about her health since walking through the door. Her career had always offered an escape to a place where she could see her value tangibly. She liked corporate politics and sales pitches, she was good at them. She'd been promoted and provided not just well, but very well for her family.

'Lisa?' Jack queried her attention down the line but there was a knock on the door, Adam opened it and stood at the entrance.

She nodded at him and said into the phone. 'I'll have to call you back.' She hung up on Jack and placed her phone on the desk. 'Have a seat,' she offered Adam the chair in front of her desk. 'Congratulations on your interim role.'

'It's okay, I won't stay long. Can we see you this afternoon?'

'Yes. I'm free after 3 p.m.. Who is *we* and what is this about?'

'Three of us have been selected to represent the executive committee, and it's about your conduct and the shape of your role going forward.'

'Nothing serious then?' said Lisa.

Adam smiled. 'I wouldn't put it that way myself.'

'Adam,' Lisa opened a drawer and took out a large folder. 'I hope you're prepared for the meeting.'

'Of course I'm prepared, I arranged for the exec committee and board to meet on the same evening. Like herding cats. Lots of work has gone into this.'

'Well, let me put that in perspective for you. I've had eight years to prepare for this meeting, ever since I last went on maternity leave. I've *taken my time* and I'll see you at three. You can close the door on your way out.'

Chapter 29

The first decision she had to make was where she would tell Chloe, because if it was too private Lisa would get the full force of her opinionated little sister – 'rambunctious' was their father's favourite adjective for Chloe, both as a child and as an adult – and if it was too public, she might make a scene. So Lisa chose a quiet restaurant far enough away from her office.

The anticipation of telling her sister revealed just how big a hole she had created in waiting to tell her, as if part of her own reaction to her illness was her sister's reaction and any denial would linger until Lisa had spoken to her.

When Chloe was thirty, just before Max was born, she'd left her fiancé. She didn't tell Lisa why, other than that he wasn't the one. Lisa felt bad for the fiancé but pleased her sister knew what she wanted enough to make a decision like that.

Then Chloe quit her job as a lawyer at one of the top law firms in the world, where she'd been a rising star and quickly promoted. Lisa had been almost as proud of Chloe's job as she was of her own and had been surprised when she quit. More so when Chloe told her she didn't have another job lined up and wasn't taking any interviews.

Chloe sold her flat and went travelling. She didn't meet Max until he was two.

The comparison to her own life was obvious and Chloe's change in direction away from Lisa seemingly too brittle to be repaired. Lisa was hurt as each decision Chloe made seemed to be a judgement written between the lines, but she hoped that when her sister came back, she'd get her old job back. She suspected that she was relying on their parents too. Chloe left, came back, took part-time jobs, rented a room in a flat-share. No, it hadn't been a phase; no, it wasn't the same as usual.

But the humour didn't stop. The familiarity hadn't ebbed. Slowly, Lisa had grown accustomed to the change in their relationship, not repaired, but altogether different. She was happy paying Chloe's way when they met, and Chloe didn't seem to mind that Lisa teased her about her errant ways. The aspects of Chloe's new life that had alienated Lisa were nothing to do with her. Chloe was leading her own life. Even if Lisa didn't like the reflection it cast, she allowed herself to be cautiously happy for her sister.

At various times in their lives they'd been joined at the hip and at other times they had blanked each other for months, but that had never made a difference to how close they were. Certain words in Lisa's own vocabulary could only ever be said and heard in Chloe's voice, even as Lisa said them. For instance, the cadence of a word Chloe might have said as a teenager would form Lisa's affectation of the word decades later. Opinions sharply made by her sister would become her own and their upbringing was as if bricks from one had ended up in the construction of the other – 'the girls', as their father had bundled them. And yet they had differences which pulled them apart.

The argument they'd had six months ago started out as a joke, years before. It came out of Lisa's lips, out of the blue, when she had referred to 'my emotionally distant husband' to Chloe. To think back on it now, it must have been a few years after Max was born and Lisa had felt a small but increasing distance from her husband and while Lisa and Laurence talked about it, the distance continued to grow, albeit incrementally.

The joke with Chloe evolved when Lisa and Laurence stopped talking about their marriage altogether. It became 'Larry's lack of communication'. Around that time, things for him at work hadn't been going well. One or two of his clients left him, and it was clear he wasn't going to get a promotion at his larger practice, so he set up on his own. All the while, Jack had been promoted to CEO, and Lisa was now number two and head of a team of forty or so people. Next, Chloe shortened it to 'Larry's Lack', and then finally, just *'La-Ree'*. And then six months ago, it came to a head.

'I've sat here and listened to the *bumps along the road* for years. Your *niggles*. If you think he's having an affair, you should speak to him. In fact, we both know it, you should leave him,' Chloe had said.

'I'm fine with it. Well, I'm not *fine* fine, but I'm sanguine. We have a family, we have a house, we're raising children together.'

'Don't be so emotionless, Lisa. You think that's you, but it's not. You can't just sweep this under the carpet, back to work and raising the kids. You can't work your way through this one. At least just speak to him.'

'You're right! Perhaps I should quit my job and go travelling! It's life, Chloe, and juggling it all is damn difficult. You should try it; oh, no, wait. You don't want all of that; heaven forbid anyone else leading a life that you wouldn't lead.'

'Don't make this about me. Fine, forget I said anything.'

'But it is about you, isn't it? Try building a life, why don't you. It's hard work making a home, building a career, raising children, working on a marriage. You only see what you would do and not what I'd do, and it hurts you. It kills you that I'm not doing what—'

That was when Chloe lost her patience. 'What the fuck would you know about me! For instance, did you know that I left my fiancé because he reminded me of Larry? Did you know that I only took a job in law because you were the one who encouraged me to, pressured me to be just like you? Some example that's turned out to be.'

'Take some bloody responsibility and build a life for yourself. This conversation is over.' As Lisa had stood up to leave the café, Chloe said, 'Go ahead. Push me into a fucking pond again, you psychopath.'

Those had been the last words they'd said to each other in person.

That was what Lisa was thinking about, sitting at the table in the restaurant, as she spotted Chloe waiting for the green man on the other side of the street. She had earphones in and a bobble hat on. She looked perfectly normal and calm. She looked both ways and crossed the street before the red man turned green, striding quickly to avoid getting honked at by the traffic. Maybe they were too different; maybe they were too similar.

Her sister came in, touched the arm of the maître d' and talked to him for nearly two minutes while Lisa's heart beat faster. Once her sister had had her fill of conversation she allowed him to take her to the table. It was the Chloe Show before she'd even sat down and everything that was still, vibrated.

'Bit out of my way, this restaurant, but that's fine. Mum said you have something to tell me?' and she sat down at the table. The maître d' smiled at Lisa as if to say, 'She's your problem now' and walked off.

'Sorry, excuse me?' The maître d' was pulled back into orbit. 'Please may I have a glass of the house wine? Red or white, whichever's better. Do you want one? Are we going to need a bottle?' Lisa smiled in spite of herself and Chloe continued. 'In fact, please can we see the wine list.' The maître d' replied the waiter would be with them shortly.

And then there were two, as their father called them: 'the girls'.

Chapter 30

All morning, Max ate that extra packet of Mini Cheddars, savouring the snack one by one; and then mouthfuls of mouthfuls of them, where you can barely swallow because they are so dry in the throat. All through maths, science then history the little packet sat in his pocket.

Until lunchtime, when he sat at a table in the busy calm of fifty or so hungry school children focused on unpacking their packed lunches. Opposite Max was Mo and they inspected each other's items as they took them out of the boxes, each one silently judged according to deliciousness. Out of Mo's packed lunch came an apple, which was okay, then a chicken and cheese sandwich with mayonnaise, which got a respectful nod from Max, and lastly, cucumber sticks, at which Max screwed up his face. Max took out the second packet of Mini Cheddars with slow reverence and Mo looked him in the eye with stern approval.

Max's first warning was the change in Mo's face as his eyes looked down at the table and his about-to-eat smile vanished. The next was the voice: *You don't have any friends*. Max couldn't be sure if he'd heard it out loud or just in his head because his imagination was powerful and the emotions that went with it, stifling.

It was his bully Luke speaking and he walked up to

their table. 'No-mates and his weirdo friend,' said Luke.

An idea occurred to Max then and there, and although he didn't smile, he must have had a glint in his eye because Mo frowned when he saw Max's face. Max said, 'Luke, I have a spare packet of Mini Cheddars. Would you like it?' He held up the packet.

Luke snatched it from Max and said, 'You should give me your Mini Cheddars every day.'

Luke then walked away, but Max jumped up and said, 'Actually, I don't want my other packet too. Would you like it?' At this, Luke turned around but he wasn't greeted by another packet of Mini Cheddars offered in Max's outstretched hand. Max felt a rush of adrenaline like nothing he had felt before and all from this idea in his head that took him beyond the rules, which he normally obeyed.

The force of the punch was a mystery to Max and when he recounted it later to the headmistress, he couldn't remember how hard he'd hit Luke. He did remember where, because he hit him twice: once in defence and once out of justice, on Mo's behalf.

The first punch – the one only Mo saw – was a punch in the stomach, Luke fell to the ground, winded. He struggled to breathe for a few seconds and Max was worried he'd hurt him badly. It took Luke about ten seconds to stand back up, still with strained breathing and Max standing in concern, not wanting to injure Luke seriously. The pair of them now squared up. When he got enough air back, Luke said, 'You're a coward, because people that bully are cowards. I'm telling on you. Both of you ganged up against me.'

The second punch, the one that half a dozen classmates saw, landed straight on Luke's nose, and as soon as Max saw the blood, he regretted it. But also in that split second, before the regret, he felt satisfied and brave for standing up for himself.

Chapter 31

Lisa had the opposite problem with Chloe that she did with her husband. With her sister, she longed for small talk to pad out the directness and stem the assault.

'I know you, Lisa. Spit it out. You'll feel better for it.' Her sister picked up her fork and started balancing it upright it on the end of her finger and the table.

'So,' said Lisa, 'summer plans?'

'I'm going to Glastonbury.'

'Who are you going with?'

'Current boyfriend and one other – a spare ticket, if you're interested?'

'Any other festivals?'

'Some, yes. Next question.'

'When was the last time you saw Mum and Dad?'

'Last week. They seemed well, if doddery.'

'Do I ever say that I appreciate that you see them more?'

'No, you don't, but it makes sense as I don't have children and you do.'

'The kids spent last night with them actually.'

The waiter came over with menus and Chloe started complimenting him on his tattoos, asking where his accent was from. 'This is my sister,' she said, 'we haven't seen each other for six months and the first question she asked me was, "What are my plans this summer?"' The Chloe Show went on and on.

When she'd finished with him, Chloe moved back to her sister. 'It's lovely to see you. I was worried when you called me from the disabled loo.'

'I need some legal advice.'

'We can come to that in a bit. How come the kids were with Mum and Dad?'

'Laurence and I needed a night in together, that's all.'

'Alice is at a tricky age. She was really upset, I didn't want to say over the phone—'

'—That she blames me for her relationship ending?' Lisa said jealously. 'I don't know how it's my fault, but apparently it is. She says I'm distant. It's not fair, Chloe – the amount of time and patience I've given her and she's throwing I don't know what back in my face.'

'If teenagers were rational human beings I might've had a child myself by now, but they are sociopaths. She'll come round. And for the record, she is very proud of her mother and her mother's success. She told me so.'

Lisa smiled. 'Larry said that she's just at that age.' Chloe grinned and Lisa opened up their door: 'I mean, *Lacking La-Ree*.'

'Lacking La-Ree indeed. And how's my favourite nephew?'

'Max is... not fine. He's being bullied at school, which I am kicking myself for not noticing. He's gone quiet. Quieter.'

'He's the sensitive one.'

'Laurence told him to punch the bully.'

'Oh, Jesus, Larry! He's not the sharpest tool in the box, is he. You need to tell Max that's not going to help.'

Some people paid and left, others arrived and were shown to their tables. A waiter came to take their order.

Without discussion, each sister ordered both a starter and a main course, because there was no work that was more urgent, or any part of life more pressing now that they were together. Lisa chose the wine and they talked and talked, on slower, restaurant time. Their food arrived and they ate and their plates were taken away and slowly the distance between them was filled in.

'So, what's the legal advice you need?' asked Chloe.

'It's work.'

'I suspected as much. Is it the same thing? They're still trying to take your clients from you? This amounts to an obstruction to you being able to perform your job. The phrase you need to use is *constructive dismissal*.'

'It's different now. I run the biggest, most profitable team in the firm, and I had assumed that when the CEO stood down, I'd be his replacement. He was fired yesterday. I'm up later today.'

Chloe took a deep breath and pursed her lips. 'What's really going on, Lisa? I know you too well and the only time you open up and talk about something serious like work is to avoid talking about something even more serious.'

Lisa gave a defensive smile – a yes, you're right smile. An unfortunately-yes-you-are-spot-on smile.

'You're ill, aren't you. Is it serious?'

Their parents had probably said something, but that didn't matter now. Lisa looked down, her fingers ran along the varnished grain of the wooden table. Tears formed, hung, then fell, which they did because in front of her sister, there was no hiding. She felt Chloe pulling her chair next to hers, then her sister's arm around her shoulders.

'No, can you leave the pudding, I'm sure we'll finish it. Can I have another glass of wine, please.'

Then silence. Well, silence from Chloe, which was more striking than the hum of the restaurant around them. Lisa sat there, her face down, with her sister's arm occasionally squeezing and rubbing her shoulder, demonstrating the patience within love and the time it took to show it.

Normally, Lisa would have wondered how they looked and would have thought it must be ridiculous: hunched over together, crying in a crowded restaurant. Normally, she would want to blame her sister's contagious emotions. But today Lisa was only grateful for her sister being here, right where she needed her to be. In all of space and time, their paths crossing, diverging and converging, their arguments and their jokes, they were here, as it'd been since the day Chloe was born. Each giving meaning to the other's existence.

Lisa reached out and they held hands under the table. She wondered what apologetic faces Chloe was making at passers-by, then felt her sister's cheek on her forehead, wet from tears of her own.

When she thought the time was right, Chloe asked again, 'Is it serious?'

'It's a tumour in my head. Sara's taking me for more tests. The doctor says I'm already a miracle of science.'

'You were a miracle from the moment you were born.'

They sat mostly still and let tears come until they ran out, no longer sad but empty. After a few more squeezes of the arm and much more quiet, Chloe said, 'I'm glad Sara's been there for you.'

'Will you come to the hospital in a few days, for the results? Sara will be there, so don't worry if you can't make it.'

'Of course I will.'

'I think I'm going to leave Larry, too.'

'Aha, there you have it: every cloud.'

Chapter 32

When the ordeal of telling her sister that she had terminal cancer was over and she only had to face the ordeal of having terminal cancer, she let go of Chloe's hand. Her sister moved her chair back to the other side of the little round table they had eaten lunch at and they understood a little more of each other, experiencing a little more life with each other.

They spoke about their parents. 'I told them that it was *probably terminal*,' said Lisa, 'which I suppose isn't as much of a lie as it seems. It is early days and I still have more tests. The oncologist was more hopeful than the neurologist.'

'Doctors aren't infallible, even neurologists. Where is your head at in terms of treatments? You're not going to refuse all treatment if it's incurable, are you?'

'For now, can we talk about my situation at work? Right now, I need you with your lawyer's hat on.'

'Okay. Tell me what's happening.'

'I'm being hauled up in front of the executive committee.' Lisa went through the last five days' events in the office right up to the meeting she was yet to have with Adam at 3 p.m. Chloe listened and took out a pen and paper and made notes and asked questions at the end.

Then her sister began and she used her hands as she spoke. 'Arguments like these, for constructive dismissal and/or bullying – *harassment* is the term to use – don't really boil down to fanciful arguments or finger-pointing. They boil down to dull, systematic evidence-compiling. This will be fairly open and shut.'

'And the fact that I've been actively holding back on sharing my clients?'

Chloe ran through what to say. 'I know that this will be your instinct too, but I advise that you do not mention the cancer, let alone that it's serious.' Lisa had forgotten that on one side Chloe never took herself seriously, but on the other she took life very seriously and could change from fanciful to formidable at the drop of a hat. As they left the restaurant, Lisa turned her phone back on and it rang immediately from an unknown number. It was a voice she recognised but couldn't quite place and it jabbed her chest with its finger.

'I'm sorry, who is this again? Please slow down and tell me what's going on.'

First, a sigh which sounded more like a tut-tutting, then, 'This is Mrs Smith, from St Michael's. Your son's been in a fight, which he started. We take acts of physical aggression very seriously here and your child must be removed immediately from school and pending a disciplinary hearing.' Lisa could see the chest pumped up and the finger now tapping a desk some miles away. Could life not give her a break? Was it too much to ask?

'Mrs Smith, thank you for ringing. You have called me out of the blue on a busy day at work. Please hold for a moment.'

'That sounded officious,' said Chloe.

'It is. Max was in a fight.'

'Oh, god. Want me to pick him up while you put the fire out in the office?'

'Yes, please,' then taking the phone off mute, she said into it: 'Mrs Smith? Firstly, I want to say that Max has been the victim – and he *is* the victim here – of bullying—'

'Your son has broken the nose of another student!'

'Mrs Smith,' Lisa shouted down the phone outside the restaurant, in the middle of the street, 'we are not going to have an argument over the phone. Listen to me. Mr Carter on your staff has flagged that my son is being bullied – there are two sides to this story. My sister is on her way to pick up my child and I will come into the school as soon as work permits, to speak with you, but I cannot pick him up myself. Does that work?'

'Can you not pick him up yourself?' asked Mrs Smith.

'No.'

'So be it. Max can wait outside my office.'

'Goodbye,' said Lisa, but the headmistress had already hung up.

'She sounds like a right bitch,' said Chloe.

'She is difficult, yes. You deal with this fire. I'll deal with the one in the office. Wish me luck,' said Lisa. 'Here's the key to the house. And Chloe…' She stepped over to give her a hug goodbye, 'Thanks for the advice. It was really helpful.'

They stood back from the hug and Chloe said, 'My pleasure. Firefighting time. See you at six-ish?'

'See you at six.'

Chapter 33

Three men in suits stared back at Lisa: one pin-striped, one grey, one navy. There was something timeless about the situation, as if by sitting across from Jeff and Toby, with Adam in the middle as ringleader, Lisa was experiencing an iteration that stretched all the way through history. In another age, these men in suits could have been demons, soldiers, clerks, footmen, gargoyles, monks or bishops. They were there to take what wasn't theirs, extracting from her career into theirs, when they should have been her colleagues.

Adam had a sparkle in his eyes, which was the excitement of achieving his goals, and the gleam of greed which motivated him towards them. He was close, but he wasn't there yet. The tip of Adam's tongue licked his upper lip. Chief Executive Officer was in his grasp with only her in the way. How inconvenient for him.

Lisa thought of Jack simmering away, thrown out of the office, blaming everything and everyone, but at the same time he wasn't a bitter man; he was fun-loving, charismatic and decent, a colleague she had loved working with. She felt like her fight was also partly their fight. Here was Adam in Jack's chair, ready to collect the rewards of the hard work she and Jack had put into the firm.

'Let's get this show on the road then. Jeff and Toby are here representing the rest of the executive committee. The board has signed off on that,' said Adam. He handed copies of a document to the other executives and to Lisa. 'As Interim CEO, I am dismissing you from your position at the company.' He was faux-grave as he spoke, unable to hide the glee in his moment. Lisa was taken aback because she had expected to be given notice – not fired – and it was brutal. But on the other hand, Adam was doing this far more quickly than he should, and she could take advantage of that.

Her mind went to a place it had gone to several times over the last few days: a clause in her employment contract which entitled her to life insurance. A quick guess was that even if she were fired (and not given notice), she should still be entitled to it because she'd discovered the tumour while being employed at the firm. But it was another risk around her throat. And then a panic – if she was fired, might the clause be invalidated? It was exactly the sort of wording she could imagine in an employment contract. Her back was against a wall.

'Fired? On what grounds?' Lisa asked.

'Firstly, absenteeism. It appears you have checked out somewhat. It's as simple as this: you have a very senior position in this company and we can't afford to have someone who's not entirely committed. You and I were meant to go to a pitch for an important client's business and that calls into question your commitment to your role. Will you up and leave and take your clients with you to a competitor?' He leaned forward confidently – overconfidently.

'We've been worried about you interviewing elsewhere,' said Jeff.

It was natural for Adam to want to clean house after getting rid of Jack, removing Jack's allies and installing his own, but he still needed to do it legally and for now, she was quiet, while Adam used up the ammunition he had.

'Secondly, you were asked to pool your clients with other executives of the company. You've resisted this change for a long time and the committee has decided they must be reallocated.' She imagined the committee members sifting through her client list and scrambling over her revenue, the fruits of her hard work. 'The document I've just passed you is our offer of a lump sum conditional on your attendance at client handover meetings over the next couple of months – to be paid upon the satisfactory completion of this final task.'

She said, 'I know you see my clients as lines on a spreadsheet, but these are people I know, people I've worked with in the industry. I respect them and they respect me. They're not just revenue. Handover will be difficult, especially if they know why I'm leaving.'

She scanned through the document and found the figure he was offering. She could see how Adam might argue that it was generous, but given her contribution to the firm, it was an insult. This was nearly twenty years of her life being taken away, her means of making a living.

'Lastly,' Adam continued, 'the executive committee feels the firm is going in a culturally different direction. It's fair to say you and Jack have contributed greatly over the years, but you did so with an emphasis on cold, hard drive. We want to create a more collegiate culture here, less *eat what you kill*.'

This was rich coming from the individual who'd taken her clients when she was on maternity leave. She waited for an additional point. Surely this man had something more? When nothing was forthcoming, Lisa began her defence.

'First, let me address your points. I can account for my absence for the last four working days – including missing the client pitch. Human Resources can confirm that I have a valid reason and that I should not have to explain it in the corporate environment.'

'I hope it's nothing serious,' said Jeff.

'Thank you. Second, repeated attempts were made by Jack with the executive committee over the years to pool my clients. Indeed, clients were assigned to you, Adam, during my maternity leave, and were never handed back. So, for historical reasons, I have been legitimately cautious in sharing clients.

'But at no point have I been told orally or in writing that not sharing my client base with the firm would be a sackable offence. Had I been, of course I would have shared them. To say that it is now sackable is to change the terms of my employment – unless you can point to a specific clause in my employment contract that says otherwise? If you can't, this is unfair dismissal.

'I would argue that, further, as business development is one of the key performance metrics of senior executives such as myself, handing over clients stops me from being able to perform my role. And this, arguably, is constructive dismissal.

'I can't speak to your assessment of the culture that I inspire in the workplace. I can only refer you to performance and to say that I have not, in twenty years, been made aware of any complaint against me.

'Now, I would like to make additional comments.' She reached over the desk and handed each of them a copy. 'This is my HR file.'

'I already have a copy of it,' interjected Adam.

'Correction. You have a *redacted* copy of my HR file. Because HR wouldn't release information to you that pertains to *you* within my folder.' She waited for a reaction from Adam, for his brow to furrow, his pupils to narrow.

'Speaking of complaints. I have made and documented over eight years of complaints with respect to Adam, since my maternity leave, when Adam took clients from me and did not hand them back, thus changing the nature of my role unlawfully. Specifically he was warned verbally by Jack, about using a phrase, "take your time", which he has uttered to me on over thirty occasions.

'This is coercion in the workplace. Furthermore, given that this phrase was first used when I went on maternity leave, and given that this was when Adam first took clients from my client list, I would argue it is also misogynistic, implying that time taken to give birth to my son was to his own career's advantage.

'Of course, if I were to make a formal complaint of bullying, it would come down to an internal investigation or external tribunal. But given the documented evidence over the last eight years, I feel that the outcome would be a foregone conclusion.

'As I was unable to attend the committee meeting, given the information that I'm bringing to light now, I put to the three representatives of the executive committee in front of me that the committee should meet again, in full.'

Jeff leaned back in his chair and shared a glance with Toby behind their colleague's back. Adam jeered, puffed, inflated then deflated. 'Well, you sure as shit don't have my vote. I see what you're trying to do here – playing politics, like you and Jack always did. Don't you see: this is all—'

Lisa looked over as Jeff spoke over Adam. 'Lisa is a senior executive. She should have been at the meeting last night anyway. She has my vote.'

Toby added, 'Adam, she makes a compelling argument. I would be uncomfortable second-guessing the rest of the executives here. They need to hear what she has to say, so she has my vote too.'

Lisa continued, 'In the meeting, I will put forward first, a motion that the current interim CEO is unsuitable for the permanent position, and second, that I am the natural successor to Jack, as my track record speaks for itself.

'It is incumbent on any senior employee of this firm to put the firm first. As such, I would like to state that I am indeed willing to share clients with other selected executives. I might be willing to hand over all my clients to executives so that I can focus on the role of CEO.'

Jeff and Toby sat up as she played music in their ears. They'd get what they'd wanted all along, without Adam.

'At this point in time I don't feel it's necessary to accept or reject the offer in this document.' She held up Adam's proposal. 'But I want it on record that if I do leave the firm, I will endeavour to ensure the smoothest of handovers of my clients.

'Lastly, in my HR file is a full list of incidents where I feel Adam has either coerced or taunted me. Documented evidence, as a point of reference.'

'A reference for what?' snapped Adam.

'For the sort of person you are,' said Lisa. 'And if I may say – mostly to the other representatives of the committee than to you – this whole process today has proved to me that you have neither the personality nor the eye for detail needed for leadership. Running a firm is about performance, not playing at office politics. I would encourage you, Adam, not to put yourself forward for the permanent CEO role.'

Chapter 34

The last hurdle of the day sat across another desk but also in a suit. Mrs Smith sat with a straight back, chin tucked into her neck and she had grey, tired-wiry hair. She had a blank stare for Lisa from behind glasses that framed pin-prick pupils.

The truly officious feared bureaucratic power as much as they delighted in wielding it. Lisa foresaw how the meeting would go. Even if she was inclined to clemency, Mrs Smith would not abandon the policies and procedures that made a school function, that she was beholden to.

On the same side of the desk as Lisa sat Mr Carter, in the other seat for parents that were hauled up in front of the headmistress. He sat where the father should have been sitting, Laurence's seat.

After Mr Carter's input, which was very much in Max's defence, Lisa and Mrs Smith had the same conversation that they'd had on the phone earlier that day. There was little to be done: rules could not be skirted around. Max had hit another child in the face. He was suspended and was probably going to be expelled, retaliation or not.

'Mr Carter, would you mind giving Mrs Smith and me a moment? There's another piece to the puzzle that needs to be discussed, and it's personal.' He looked surprised but deferential as he excused himself and left the office.

'Mrs Smith, last Thursday, I went to see my local GP, a university friend of mine who is my family's GP. I was supposed to pick up some test results – nothing serious. The results, from a CT scan, were that I have a brain tumour. I saw the neurologist yesterday, who said it's likely that I have a matter of months to live, but it could well be less.

'I am very worried about my children, my teenage daughter as well as Max. They will need compassion more than ever and school will be a necessary refuge for my son given the horrors that await him. I am sorry to put this at your feet, but it's important. Max and my daughter, Alice, don't know yet.'

Mrs Smith started writing notes. 'I'm sorry. I'm very sorry. But by tomorrow, every student in the school *and their parents* will know that your son broke another child's nose. I don't know what you think I can do about that. We can refer to mitigating circumstances in his dismissal report, but he must be dismissed. I have you and Mr Carter saying that it was provoked, but the boy himself says that Max was the bully. What am I to do exactly, other than expel him too?'

Lisa felt the strain on her forehead, the psychological spilling over into the physical: an intense headache right in the front of the brain, far away from the tumour. It was a headache just for Mrs Smith. 'Put the shoe on the other foot. My son was being bullied – as noted by Mr Carter – and nothing has been done. You say you have a zero-tolerance policy? Then the school is at fault for not applying zero tolerance where my son was concerned. The other child should have been reprimanded before it came to a head. My son has never been accused of bullying and has always behaved well. What's the point of good behaviour if, when something like this comes along, he doesn't receive the benefit of the doubt? Max deserves it.'

The headmistress's face ticked slightly to the right as if her neck were made of cogs and not of muscle. 'What benefit of the doubt do you want? Several people saw him punch the other child, while no one – not even your son – has complained about the other child. There is no doubt that he attacked another student and I am in the unenviable position of enforcing the rules.'

'Unenviable position.' The words stuck. What could be more unenviable than her own position? Lisa sat back and stared blanky into nothing because there was nothing she could do. There was one last thing for it, one small hope for her little boy to stop all this. 'It's not Max's fault. When my husband found out our son was being bullied, he told him to punch the boy bullying him. Please don't expel him. Do anything else, but not expulsion. It's my husband's fault.'

'I am sorry, Lisa.' The headmistress paused, and Lisa held her breath in hope. They sat there for a while, Lisa hoping for compassion. Then Mrs Smith's neck ticked again, and she looked directly at Lisa. 'I truly am sorry, but I can't run a zero-tolerance school for some and not others.' The headmistress looked down at her desk, ashamed.

'Don't you have any compassion?'

Mrs Smith prodded a piece of paper on her desk. 'I don't have the luxury of compassion. It was my duty to ensure your child was safe and happy and that clearly wasn't the case. I will come down hard on both children, you have my word.'

'What will happen to the other child?'

'Luke? If I can find confirmation that he has been bullying Max, he will be suspended, but as it wasn't physical, it will not be expulsion. If Max says he was physically mistreated as well, that's another question.'

After that, Lisa spoke her mind, 'I don't think there's anything more we need to discuss. I don't want my son in your school.'

Chapter 35

Inside a marriage can be irritation or exasperation or anger, even hate. There is a mountain of things that may be going on. Niggles worm their way deeper until they settle as contempt. Never had Lisa gone into her home with the absolute certainty of confrontation. Things had come to a head, things had been neglected, things had been allowed to fester unsaid, and she was fucking angry with her husband.

What was Laurence thinking? Punch the bully? Brash Laurence, who gave advice without thinking. Stupid Laurence, who resorted to violence. Simple Laurence, who spoke in clichés. Inattentive Laurence, who parented without thought. Spoiling Laurence, who gave the children whatever they wanted. Deceitful Laurence, who blamed her for their distance. Frustrated Laurence, whose career hadn't panned out as it had promised to. Unfulfilled Laurence, who looked outside their marriage. Lost Laurence, who couldn't let go of his marriage.

She turned off the engine and ran through what she'd say to him, how she'd say it, which things she'd bring up from the past to hurt him if he resisted. She felt waves of physical anger. She got out of the car and the cold spring night air sobered her up. She reminded herself that her job was now secure, that Chloe was coming to the hospital, that Laurence still didn't know she was ill.

Lisa heard little footsteps running upstairs and Max stood looking down the stairway for her reaction, searching her face for the anger he thought he deserved. He would have seen her parking the car outside, and had been waiting and watching for her from his window. He had swollen eyes and a runny nose and when she smiled at him his face crunched up quietly.

Lisa sat at the bottom of the stairs and opened her arms. He walked down step by step, holding on to the banister. When they were level they hugged and for a moment it was just the two of them in each other's arms, a mother and a son. And that's all there was, or ever would be.

Chapter 36

Through the doorway into the kitchen, like looking through a keyhole that was the size of the door itself, Lisa saw Chloe with a large glass of white wine. Then she saw her husband leaning back on the counter. He walked over to her and put his arms around her. 'I am so sorry, pet. I am so sorry.'

'Don't call me *pet*,' said Lisa.

For the first time in a long while, wrapped up in his apology, she felt genuine support from her husband, albeit support that was an apology based on guilt, which was exactly the support she didn't want from him. And with a nickname – 'pet' – that condescended and infantilised, even dehumanised.

She was end-of-the-day tired, a day when her son had been expelled and she'd nearly got fired. She caught her own breath as she realised it was a day when both she and Max had confronted their bullies. For a moment she was pleased with Laurence and happy that Max had stood up for himself. She hugged her husband back and put her ear on his chest. Then the moment passed and she went to the fridge and joined them in a glass of wine, sitting down next to her sister at the table.

'Cheers,' said Chloe holding up her glass. 'To finding Max a better school without such a cow of a headmistress.'

'Cheers to that,' said Laurence.

'Did you go in too?' asked Lisa.

'I did. Too late to pick Max up, but I spoke to Mrs Smith. Probably not the time to say it, but I would have liked to have punched her.'

'That's the spirit, La-Ree,' said Chloe.

Lisa choked on her wine and when she'd finally stopped coughing, she asked, 'How was Max?'

'In floods of tears when I picked him up. But we went for an ice cream and that cheered him up a bit.' said Chloe. 'Then I set him up with Sebastian and his Nintendo on the sofa and we chatted until Larry came back. He can eat toast, you know that? Anyway, on that note, I think my work here is done, so I'll leave you both to it.'

'Thank you for being a great aunt,' said Laurence.

'*Thank you* for the glass of wine,' said Chloe.

Lisa walked Chloe to the door. In the hallway, Chloe said, 'Your house looks lovely.'

'I know, it's been a while since you were last here. It won't be so long next time.'

Lisa was in a good mood, given all that had happened. It was good to have her sister back in her house. It was good to have work, if not sorted, then not such a worry. She felt playful. She said, 'Mum and Dad are worried about you, Chloe.'

'Pipe down.'

'We were talking. They want you to find someone and settle down.'

'Stop it.'

'In fact, Mum and I were talking and we think you should do a course. Something to focus on.'

'Right! Love you, bye!' Chloe opened the front door.

'I'll see you the day after tomorrow, at the hospital,' Lisa said quietly.

Her sister was out the door, both feet on the garden path, when she turned round and said in a whisper, 'Stay strong. Fingers and toes crossed for the results. And good luck with La-Ree tonight.'

Chapter 37

'Your sister seems well.'

'I hadn't seen her in far too long. I hope you didn't mind me sending her to pick Max up. She's been there for Alice too. I'm very grateful to her.'

'What do you mean, *she's been there for Alice*?'

They were standing in the kitchen, and it seemed to Lisa that they didn't have anything to say to each other. There was no real reason for them to speak. Laurence was leaning back against the kitchen worktop by the sink, Lisa against the fridge. It was awkward, similar to conversation on a first date. Who was going to make the first effort to get to know the other? Lisa said, 'Alice and Chloe talk quite a bit.'

'About what?'

'I don't know, Larry, I'm not on their calls. I suppose, about her break-up. Possibly about us, because Alice is worried about our marriage, her family.'

'Our daughter is like that. She puts everything on herself. I was thinking we could go away somewhere for the weekend. A cheap city break or a cottage somewhere in the countryside.'

'Why? So Alice can stop worrying?'

'Don't be obnoxious. Obviously for us.'

'Maybe. I've got a lot on at the moment, but it could be fun for the kids to be looked after by Chloe. The timing's not great, with work and everything else. Maybe further down the line.' Was he suggesting a weekend away just so that, when the time came, he could say, *at least I tried*?

'Yeah, in a month. So, what happened at work?'

'I don't want to talk about it, but I don't think there's a problem anymore.'

'You settled the dispute? Or have you decided to search for a new job? I wish I could have been there. You're incredible in situations like that.'

'Adam is on the back foot and I'll make him an offer before the executive committee meet at the end of the week.'

'What offer?' asked Laurence.

'I haven't decided. When is Alice back?'

'She texted to say she'll be home in an hour. But what offer did they make you?'

'I'd like to speak to her alone this evening and if it's okay, can we have the house to ourselves? There's something wrong with our relationship and I need to fix it.'

'I think I should be there too.'

'I was hoping you could take Max out for dinner, cheer him up with a burger or something.'

'Whatever it is between you and Alice, it'd be good if I'm there, especially as she and I are close at the moment. It'll help smooth things over.'

'And how exactly would you do that? Tell me honestly: what were you and Alice really talking about at the bus stop?'

'Why are you going on about that? I told you, it was her allowance or something. I can't remember.'

Laurence, still leaning against the counter, walked over to the table and refilled his glass of wine, then went back to his perch against the kitchen worktop. Lisa sat at the table and filled her own glass. 'No, enough is enough. I want my daughter back and I've got important things to tell her, so I'm asking for the house to ourselves.'

'Enough is enough? There you go again, making *important* decisions without me and telling our daughter *important* things that you keep me locked out from. What things? Don't you think as your husband, I should know anything *important* and if we're going to work on our marriage, we should start with being more open?'

Lisa looked him square on. 'I think, given the day Max has had, that I'm entitled to take my own advice on parenting. I don't want an argument, so let's not go down this path.'

She was almost ready to say it now, her emotions were crystallising into words. For better for worse, for richer or poorer, in sickness and in health? *But you weren't there for me in health, so I won't let you be here for me in sickness.* Lisa wasn't ready yet. 'I'd like to buy Max a PlayStation, or games for his Nintendo, or whatever he wants,' she said.

'Where's this coming from?'

'I'd like to do that. It's important to me.'

'*Important*. There we go again. No. He's just been expelled for hitting someone. We're not going to reward that behaviour.'

'Which he did because you said he should.'

Laurence shouted with the tone of a male scream, not in frustration, but anger. The kind that made sensitive children anxious and shameful. Children like Max upstairs in his bedroom. He said, 'But I didn't say he should be fucking rewarded for it, did I!'

Lisa let their bodies talk because she didn't want to speak after being shouted at. That she was sitting down and he was standing up; that he had shouted and she had spoken. When he understood this, when his shoulders relaxed and his jaw was not lowered forward, she said calmly, 'I will give you this: you've never shouted at me before. But I don't think you should ever shout at me again. I'll ask you not to because Max will blame himself if he thinks we're arguing about him.'

'Why do you make these things up just to control the conversation? All these little things you make up when you want to win an argument. It's insufferable.'

'I don't make these things up, Laurence. He's a sensitive boy and he'll blame himself if he hears us arguing, so let's not get into a shouting match.'

Lisa watched her husband calm himself down. She watched each marker, each piece of body language throw in the towel, each turn of the head and squint of the eye admit he should not have shouted at her, recognising he had no need to be there when she spoke with their daughter.

'I'm going to have a shower. We'll be back by eight thirty or nine. Tomorrow, you and I need to look for new schools.'

'Thank you, Laurence. I'll ring around for some day care too.'

'Don't mention it.'

In the not-too-distant future was the conversation about private school and whether Max should go to one. The last time they'd discussed this, they'd decided that there was no need because the state schools were good nearby, but Laurence had been more keen on the idea. Looking back on it now, and the repeat of the conversation in the future, Lisa couldn't remember if it had been her opinion that Max shouldn't go or the fact that she'd be paying for it that meant she'd had the final word over Laurence. She let this go. Right now it wasn't important.

What had stopped her from saying to Laurence that she was sick and that she didn't want to spend the rest of her life married to him? The whole world could be seen through a new lens, but it might take a nudge or it might take a decade of lessons learned, one on top of the other stacking up, so that a higher vantage point is a new perspective. What was meaningful and what held little value could all change place in an instant or at the end of a long road. There were still things she needed to do before she asked him for a divorce. She needed to know more about possible treatments, and she needed to tell her daughter.

When Laurence came downstairs his hair was wet and he was in tracksuit bottoms with their son behind him holding Sebastian. He reported in that they were going to drive a little further to Max's favourite burger place. He *reported in*, already as if he was someone else to Lisa, someone who co-parented with her, met with her, exchanged parenting information, then moved on.

'Are you hungry, darling?' asked Lisa.

'Yes, I want a large chips.' Max looked up at his father.

'If you ask Dad nicely, he might even let you have a milkshake. Sorry I can't come too.'

'Why can't you and Al come too?' asked Max.

'Well, sometimes grown-ups need to spend time alone catching up, and I haven't done that with your sister for a long time and she is a grown-up now, as you will be too, sooner than you think.'

Max put Sebastian down and the dog made a beeline for the sofa Lisa was sitting on. Laurence picked up his son and kissed him as if he were no bigger than a toddler. 'You're almost too big for me to do that, aren't you?' he said.

They put their shoes on in the hallway, talking about what they were going to eat, should the fries have cheese on top, should they order pickles on their burgers. Laurence told Max to put on his jacket and take a scarf. It was a package of parenthood, a cacophony of noise and discussion that went into bringing Max up into adulthood. She might soon no longer contribute to it but, Lisa hoped, wherever she was, she'd be able to hear it.

The clank-cling of the lock opened, followed by the squeeze of the hinges and the bang-shut behind them. Outside, Laurence would continue talking to Max, continue the parenting Q&A that went with the mind of a curious eight-year-old. Lisa sat on the sofa, happy to have the house to herself.

A moment later she heard a key slide into the lock. 'Mum?'

'In here.'

'Just chatted to Max and Dad in the car,' said Alice. 'What do you want to talk about? How come I'm not getting a burger?'

Chapter 38

Lisa came back into the living room with a bottle of wine and two glasses. 'I'd offer you a glass now, but first we need to speak with a clear head.'

Alice sat in the sofa chair opposite.

'You know—' Lisa stopped, letting a wave crash over her face which she kept like rock and stone because now was the time to keep it together. 'You know, moments like these are so special. For me to spend time with you, just the two of us.' Another wave hit her, this time crashing not just over but through the rock. Her face crumpled up and tears fell.

'Mum?' Alice stood up and sat next to her, throwing her weight into the hug like only a lanky teenager could do. It gave Lisa all the more love and all the more worry. She cried a little more.

'What's wrong? Tell me.'

'Okay, let me just pour the wine first,' Lisa caught her breath as she filled up each glass. She put the bottle down then looked forward into the distance. How was she supposed to do this?

'Do you remember that I blacked out a few weeks ago?' She wondered if she shouldn't just close her eyes and say what she had to say to get it out of her. Then open them, onto a new world in which her daughter knew her mother had cancer.

That would be much easier, but she kept eye contact, and her daughter nodded. 'I had a CT scan, and it was the results from that that I was picking up that day the other week. Apparently – and I say *apparently* because I feel fine, absolutely fine – I have a tumour in the middle of my brain. The likelihood is that it's inoperable. It's already quite large.'

'Mum?'

'Let me finish. Your dad doesn't know yet. I wanted to tell you first because you're an adult. You're my child but you're also an adult now.'

Lisa picked up her glass of wine. She wanted to say, 'Here's to the seventeen years I got with you' but in the moment, that felt too dark, but nor was she happy with, 'Death is part of life, darling,' which was what she did say. Alice said nothing and hugged her mother.

Then followed a thousand sympathies and questions and the waves crashed upon both of their faces and Lisa explained that she was – medically – already a walking miracle, but there were still more tests to be taken and then there would be side effects and so on.

*

Eventually, lines were drawn through dots joining to form a picture and Alice said, 'So, Granny and Grandpa know? She said we needed to be there for you. Granny can be quite stern when she wants to be, can't she?'

'Yes, she was a very different mother to how she is as a grandmother.'

'Mum?'

'Yes?'

Alice sat up. 'Why haven't you told Dad?'

Lisa picked up the other wine glass and offered it to her daughter. 'That's what this is really for.'

Chapter 39

'I know you're scared about the prospect of your dad and I separating, and it feels wrong that we're having this conversation when your dad and I haven't agreed to separate. But I needed to tell you about the cancer first and our separation is wrapped up in it.

'Obviously, it goes without saying we love you both very much. And to some extent, each other too. I can't tell you exactly when it started, but we drifted apart, and that changed the reality of our marriage. Sorry, darling, I don't think it's appropriate for me to tell you anything more than this.'

'Are you going to get divorced?'

'That still sounds very final to me. We'll separate first and go from there.'

There were parts of the story she wanted to tell Alice, bits that she felt her daughter was old enough to hear, but Lisa was conscious of a very real line keeping their children out of what was between her and her husband.

'I don't understand, Mum. Why now, when you need all the support you can get?'

As ever, her daughter found the kernel of the issue. Lisa thought hard about the answer to this. Choosing her words carefully, she said, 'When I say we've drifted apart, that's only one way of saying it. Another is that I have been completely alone inside our marriage. I don't know how long… maybe months, maybe years… And who knows, maybe your dad feels alone too. When we're ready, we'll speak to you and Max.'

'I understand. I'm sorry you felt like that, Mum.'

*

As her mother continued, Alice was quiet as she listened, quiet as her world expanded that little bit more. On the one hand, her mother made sense. It was a decision reached on a fair emotional basis – she was alone in her marriage. She saw her mother's point of view and was proud of her that she could voice it. On the other, Alice's family was breaking up and she saw a future of her father living in one house and her mother living in another. And then later, only her father alive.

The place where her mother's illness met her parents' separation both made sense and left questions. Then it clicked: Alice realised she'd expected them to separate, and that was why she'd been so angry. 'Mum, is there someone else? I wouldn't blame you if there was. I can handle it. I'd understand.' *I don't blame Dad.* Alice felt guilty for saying this because she did actually blame her father, maybe even as much as her mother, but for some reason, it had been her she'd wanted to hurt.

'No, of course not,' Lisa blinked at her daughter. 'What makes you say that?'

'Nothing,' she said a little too quickly. 'You mean, no one else? I'm not angry, I'd just like to know if that's the case.'

'No one, darling. If there had been, I wouldn't have felt so alone, would I?'

'I don't know…' Alice trailed off, making more connections in her own head. So it was just her father, then. 'So, you're leaving Dad. But why haven't you told him that you're sick? What's that got to do with the state of your marriage?'

'I don't think it's a case of me not telling him. Believe it or not, I'm not trying to hurt him. I will tell him, just not now.'

Alice pressed her again. 'I don't understand. You're together, and you're raising kids together. I'm not criticising...'

'Darling, if I told him now, he would want to support me and I don't want his support in the context of a marriage. We need to separate first, or at least agree to it, and then I can tell him.' Alice gave her mother more silence, more room to open up, more lines to fill. 'I love your father, but not romantically and even if he doesn't realise it, it's the same for him, too. I don't want his affection because I'm ill when he's already withdrawn from me. It would be utterly synthetic and performative. I have you and Max. I have Chloe and Sara. The ones I love and who love me back. There'll be a place for your dad in my life, but it won't be as my husband. Don't be worried or scared – your dad and I will work it out together.'

'I'm not scared, or worried, Mum…' said Alice pausing dramatically, 'I'm actually hungry. Really, really hungry.'

They left the living room and went into the kitchen, followed by Sebastian. Alice opened the fridge and the two of them inspected the offerings inside.

'Spag bol?' suggested Lisa. Alice hugged her, put her head on her mother's chest, and nodded.

*

The sauce was homemade and had been in the fridge for a week, Lisa had made a large batch and frozen the rest.

An idea occurred to her, 'Can you wait a little longer for dinner?' Alice looked back at her mother quizzically. 'It's literally five minutes out of our way.' Lisa opened the freezer door and took out the two jars of bolognese sauce. 'Hold these. Come on. It'll be fun. Get your nice new coat.'

She led her daughter down the street. 'Mum they're too cold to carry.' Lisa looked over and saw the jars had frosted up.

'Put them in your coat pocket. Come on, we're almost there.'

'Where are we going?'

'Right… here.' She couldn't remember with certainty which number Bill was on their street. She'd felt sorry for him that night in the park and had a sudden urge to help him, to acknowledge the moment when they'd shared their own isolations. And maybe now, because she'd managed to tell her daughter about her own loneliness, she had the impulse to help someone else. She knocked on his door – there was no bell – and wondered when he'd last had home-cooked food. The hallway light flicked on through the glass in the front door and a shape got bigger as it approached the door.

'Mum,' Alice whispered, 'who lives here?'

Bill opened the door and his face was apologetic as he saw Lisa and Alice. 'Hello, Bill,' said Lisa, smiling, 'I hope we're not disturbing you. This is my daughter, Alice.' She wondered if he remembered her from the park bench.

'Hello,' said Alice.

'Hello,' he said, then to Lisa anxiously, 'how are you? Are you okay?'

'Yes, very much better, or at least, better given the circumstances. I know this is out of the blue, knocking on your door. I wanted to introduce my daughter. Bill is our neighbour, I met him recently walking Sebastian. Anyway, we were just about to cook dinner and I remembered we had loads extra in the freezer and I thought you might like some.' She realised she'd forgotten to bring pasta to have it with. 'Sorry, I didn't bring any pasta.'

'That's very kind of you, thank you. I have pasta.' Alice handed over the jars, 'Oh, they're cold!' He stood there, holding a jar in each hand clearly unsure what to say.

What Lisa wanted to say was that she was dealing with things. She wanted to say that even though Max had been expelled, at least now he wasn't getting bullied. She wanted to say to Bill that she had told people about her tumour. She wanted to say that she was going to leave her husband and that she was happy, for the first time in a long while. It surprised her, but she also wanted to ask if he'd maybe seen her husband with a woman, but Alice was there. 'Anyway, I wanted to pop by and say hello, and the next time I'm walking Sebastian and I see a light on, I might knock on your door and see if you want to join me.'

'That would be lovely. Yes,' he said, stiffening his back, 'please do. Why don't you take my number?' Lisa took out her phone and he dictated it.

'Okay, then,' said Lisa.

'Bye, Bill. Nice to meet you,' said Alice.

'Good evening. Have a lovely dinner,' he said, closing the door gently.

Halfway down the street, Alice asked, 'Who's he?'

'I know it was a little out of the blue, but I had a sudden urge to do something nice for him. He's an old man who needs a bit of company, even if that's just to see a friendly face once in a while. He doesn't have anyone.'

Back in the kitchen, they heated up the bolognese from the fridge while the spaghetti boiled in water, Lisa grated parmesan and Alice laid the table for two. They talked more about the new future now opening up in front of them. Sharing questions and making observations.

'How are you going to tell Max?'

Lisa put two plates of spaghetti bolognese down, along with a bowl of grated cheese. Alice poured them another glass of wine each and made a little fuss of lighting a candle. 'I don't know. How do you tell an eight-year-old this?' said Lisa.

'We should tell him together. Maybe even with Dad, after you tell him. If you're comfortable with that?'

'I think that's a very good idea. We'll do it like that, the four of us as a family.'

'I love you, Mum.'

'Don't. I'll start crying and lose my appetite. Anyway, I still have to have more tests. You never know.'

'More tests?'

'To see what treatments are available. I'm seeing the oncologist in a few days with Sara.'

'You know Aunt Chloe misses you, Mum.'

'I had lunch with her today and she's coming to the hospital. You should come too.'

'Of course I will.'

They sat down at the table, food ready and table laid. They were hungry, so they were quiet as they ate, passing over salt and pepper in silence with only the sound of cutlery on porcelain. It was peaceful and the opposite of dinner with Laurence the night before. After a while Lisa asked, 'Can I ask, what happened with your break-up? Was the boy at your school?'

Alice was quick as she talked, perhaps relieved to talk about something else. 'It was awful, Mum. He put so much on me in the break-up, kind of like a character assassination. He told me why he didn't think it would work, and broke down all the things he didn't like about me: my friends, what I wear, my personality.'

'That's pathetic. Like what?'

'I pride myself on being empathetic, whether that's being aware of how a friend is feeling, or standing up for someone who's being bullied, or checking in on the Bills of the world. And yet, he said I wasn't affectionate, that I had weird boundaries he had to keep second-guessing.'

'Go on.'

'Like, I wanted to take things slowly and he was quite intense. He was always trying to move the conversation to *us*, talking about us as a couple, how we were working out as a couple, talking about our future after school. I thought it was sweet at first, then I found it cloying.'

'Can I ask, how physical was your relationship?'

'It was physical.'

'That can be intense at your age, and confusing.'

'It wasn't just that. He was very touchy-feely, always having his arm around me in breaks or holding hands. Like, whenever we were in the same room.'

'It sounds as if he needed constant affirmation because he was insecure. From the way you're speaking about him it sounds like you weren't far away from breaking up with him. Closer than you think, perhaps.'

'Yeah,' said Alice, 'maybe.'

'Do you want to know what it sounds like? It sounds as though he seems like a nice boy, is probably quite popular, or at least friendly with everyone, and I bet that's one of the things that attracted you to him. But – and it's a big "but"– while he's aware of other people's emotions, he's not so aware of intimate emotions. Therefore, he's better socially and worse in a relationship. And somewhere in the middle are his own emotions, wants and desires. And no matter how nice he tries to be, he prioritises them. And he doesn't just prioritise them, like breaking up with you rather than working out differences; he holds his emotions above everything and everyone, so that as far as he's concerned, you had to be beholden to them. He was insecure because you weren't beholden. That's why he said what he did when he broke up with you... He had to take you down a peg.'

'Can you explain?'

'I want you to hear it from me and even if you don't accept it, you should hear it.'

'Say it,' said Alice.

'What he said to you was cruel. It takes a cruel person – no matter how superficially kind they are – to say what he said. Not because he broke up with you – that happens all the time and I'm sure along the way, you'll be the one breaking up with boys – but because he had to get his lines in first and say that it was your fault. Because "nice" boys don't do the breaking up, they imply that you forced them to do it somehow.'

Alice had a brave face on but her creased chin gave her away. 'And then I found out that he'd been cheating on me.' She was quiet, she put her fork down and could only glance at her mother. Lisa wondered if Alice understood what she'd just said but she was confident that Alice would get it soon enough, it just had to sink in. 'He was cheating on me,' said Alice again, staring at her plate of food.

'I'm sorry, darling.' They weren't halfway through their pasta but neither ate any more. It felt foolish to eat in this place, where the conversation had led them. Lisa said, 'How did you find out?'

'We broke up and my friends got round me. One of them heard that he was going out with another girl already, like, *the next day*. I didn't know his new girl well – different social group. Eventually it came out they'd been seeing each other for a week.'

'The playground grapevine. Oh, darling I'm sorry. Do you think people knew before you did?'

'No, it's not that.'

'What is it then?' She saw her daughter getting more upset, so drew her chair round and sat down next to her, her arm around her daughter's shoulders, like Chloe's in the restaurant around her own shoulders, earlier that day. 'It's been a tough day,' said Lisa.

'Mum, please don't be angry.'

'Oh, darling. What is it?'

'I didn't want to say anything. A few weeks ago, I saw Dad leaving home with someone, a woman your age. Dad and I spoke about it. Maybe I should have said something to you earlier, but I didn't know what to do. He said it was just an architect and they were having a meeting. I called bullshit and he started off on me, shouting "How dare I" and "Only a child could be so naive and pathetic to jump to such a conclusion"... and how much it would upset you if I said anything.' Lisa took it all in as Alice continued, 'Then on the way to school, at the bus stop, I called bullshit again and said he had to tell you. I called him a coward. We almost had a screaming match in the street, but then he came clean. He said you knew about it and that you were trying to work on it... Mum, he implied you were having an affair too – like, an open marriage. I didn't know who to talk to. I wanted to talk to Chloe, but somehow, I couldn't tell her either.'

There it was: *I don't blame Dad.* Lisa made a snap decision that she wouldn't draw her daughter into her marriage any further than Laurence already had. 'I won't say anything to him, darling. I've suspected it for a while but believe it or not, it's not why I'm going to leave him. The affair is more a symptom of the other stuff.' It gave her more resolve to separate from Laurence. More resolve, and more certainty.

Chapter 40

Like water around a rock, life flowed around sickness and the end of a marriage and nothing changed and like normal, like always, when they'd finished their dinner Alice and Lisa cleared the table and put the dishes into the washing machine and left bowls and spoons out for breakfast. They decided to start a movie before the boys got back.

'You haven't seen *Pretty Woman*?'

'No, who's in it?'

'Julia Roberts?'

'Who?'

Their conversation went back to normal, absurdly normal, while the calamity of what they had been discussing started to land. At some points, Lisa could watch the movie and at others, the TV might as well have been a mile away.

*

Alice sat on the sofa chair, across from her mother and to the side, she took out her phone and texted her aunt: *Mum told me her news*.

A few seconds later, she saw the dots that showed Chloe was typing: *Are you okay*?

Alice replied: *I'm shell shocked. I don't think it's sunk in yet. She's going to leave Dad, too.'* Alice wondered if she should mention the stuff about the affair but she decided her mother could do that when she was ready to. They had a brief conversation:

Call me ANY TIME you want
I'm coming to the hospital with you, Sara and Mum
Of course you are, you wonderful human being
See you then x x
Amanhã x

*

The boys came back and Laurence took Max straight to bed. He came down ten minutes later.

'I started reading him a bedtime story but he went out like a light. Poor boy.'

'Shhh, Dad. Be quiet and watch,' said Alice.

You guys get paid on commission, right? Big mistake... Big, big mistake.

Laurence put himself down on the sofa near but not next to Lisa. In her head a clock started to tick and watching the film became harder and the ticking louder and louder as time went on. Eventually there was no use waiting any longer. The film had become background noise behind the ticking of the clock and she said, 'Darling, it's almost ten o'clock and it's a school night. I think it's bedtime, don't you?'

'There's not much longer left,' said Laurence.

*

Alice stood up with a jolt. 'Night, Mum,' she said, leaning in with a kiss. A kiss that was now an expression of a daughter treated like an adult, and a mother back in her daughter's confidence. Touch was once again part of their conversation, as if a mother and daughter who touched each other could only ever say the truth to each other. Touch was truth for Alice and in front of her father, she demonstrated this truth by sharing a kiss goodnight, a secret hidden from him.

But there was another secret, one which she hid from her mother. The secret inside not saying goodnight to her father and the anger that was now firmly placed on him. What her father had said to her to keep her quiet, to shift the blame onto her mother. Pennies dropping. Lenses changing. Paradigms shifting. Anger burning.

*

Once they heard Alice's footsteps above them, Laurence said, 'Looks like you two have made up.'

'We had a heart-to-heart. It's a relief to have no more surliness.' No more hard eyes. 'We talked about what was going on for her at school and her break-up. It's so much tougher being a teenager today than it was in our time. I worry about Max when it's his turn. How was dinner?'

'There is nothing that a burger can't fix for an eight-year-old boy. He ate everything. You should have seen him – nuggets, milkshake. But we talked about what happened at school. Lisa, the bullying has been going on for a long time. He feels guilty about hitting the other child, but he feels worse about his punishment. I tried to bring up different schools but he doesn't want to leave his friends.'

Laurence pressed play and the film continued, which hurt Lisa – his continuation of their evening as if that was that, said and done. She tried to follow suit, back to the movie. But while the last of the film played Lisa heard the ticking clock again. How could Laurence not hear that? It drowned out the film as it drowned out her thoughts. She turned up the volume on the TV until Laurence gave her a look. How come Laurence wasn't saying 'Can you hear that?' when it was bursting Lisa's eardrums. She looked up at the ceiling, then over to Laurence. Now he was looking up at the ceiling too and neither of them were watching the TV. An ocean apart on the same sofa.

'Laurence, can we talk?'

'Sure, what's up?' he said so simply, in a breath so seamless it seemed he'd been ready for her question his whole life. He picked up the remote, turned off the TV and turned to face Lisa.

She didn't know what she wanted to say or what words she should use. Should she confront him about the woman Alice had seen? She wanted a manual for break-ups and a manual for motherhood, and once she'd read them, manuals for life and death too.

'Something's wrong, isn't it?' she began.

She waited for him to get his first gripe in, to say, 'Wrong with what?' or 'Yeah, you asked me if I was cheating on you.' But he said nothing.

So, she said everything in one go: 'We don't talk beyond small talk; we aren't here for each other unless it's to do with the kids. Saying it now makes me think that I don't even need to say it – that we've got to a point where it's so obvious that if you can't see it, then what we have really is over, because you really don't know me at all.'

'Wait,' he said. 'So, on the one hand, if I see *it*, then we're in agreement that we what – get divorced? – and on the other, if I don't see *it*, then there's no point in being together anyway? Can we take a step back and just acknowledge that there're two people in this marriage.'

'Of course there are two in this marriage, but... Let me put it another way: either you can see that I'm alone in this marriage and have done nothing about it, or you can't see that I'm adrift and it's on me to do something about it... which is what I'm doing now.'

He shook his head. 'I don't want to break this family up. I like our life and I think things aren't so bad as to be unfixable. Why are these feelings coming out now, if you say it's been years in the making? Answer me honestly: was this something you discussed with Alice?'

'No.'

'Tell me the truth,' he said.

'I am. We didn't discuss this and I think we should leave the children out of this.'

'I think it's fair to say you shouldn't have let this build up. And it's fair that we talk this through first. Fine, there's distance between us, but fair is deciding what to do *together*. I say let's work on it and I bet in a month's time we will be fine.'

'Fair? Fairness doesn't come into it. We're talking about emotions.'

'Yeah, okay. Fine. Emotions and a relationship; a marriage; a home; our children... I feel you're making decisions about all those things on your own. And when you say, *fairness doesn't come into it*, well, that says it all to me. This is all coming from you.'

'Then I accept it's all coming from me. If you need to do that, blame me. What are we going to do next?'

'I need a drink.' He stood up and left Lisa on the sofa, made himself a drink in silence then sat back down. 'What about last night?'

'What about it? We had sex, there wasn't any connection. It only confirmed to me how I feel.'

'Why don't we try and work it out?'

'You just said it's all my fault, so I think you mean, why don't *I* try and work it out?'

'Oh, fucking hell. Don't put words into my mouth.'

'Do you really want to try and fix this? Look how far we are from each other. It makes no sense.'

'And how have you reacted exactly? If we are that distant, why are you only now saying something? Have you been gunning for us to fail, letting our relationship get to a point where there's no turning back? Do you realise how cruel it is to hear that the last years of our marriage have all meant nothing?'

She waited for him to continue, to let it out. What could she say? It was on him. He was the battleground, the scorched earth where this conversation needed to be had. Sympathies rose inside her at some points but were sunk by his blaming of her and her anger that he'd put it on Alice to keep his affair secret. She felt a sudden urge to tell him what Alice had told her, that she knew. It would make this conversation a lot quicker, but she had to protect her daughter.

Maybe her desire to separate was out of the blue, but also, it wasn't, and second-guessing herself on his behalf only made her realise how deeply self-doubt had set in, and the shame in the self-doubt she now felt when she looked back on the last year. On the other side of the coin, was Laurence capable of doubting himself?

Her cancer was out of the blue. Her resolve had arrived with it and that was enough for her. But the state of their marriage? The distance? The affair? That he'd had the indiscretion to stage his affair in their house?

'And how dare you suggest that I'm cheating on you,' he said, 'like you did last night. As if to win an argument. It's very like you, Lisa, to put these arguments out ahead, laid down in advance, in readiness for this conversation. It's calculating. Don't think I don't see it. You know, I've always felt like second fiddle in this marriage and I guess this is the perfect example. You're ready to move on, so off you go.'

Oddly, now, it was easy to keep their daughter out of it. 'I don't believe the man I married could be this isolated from me without being closer to someone else. We didn't make it all the way, Laurence. That's okay – lots of people don't. But I'm not going to spend,' *possibly my last* 'six months trying to put it all back together again.'

She watched him very closely for his reactions and cues. Knowing him this well was her way of subverting his anger. Instead of rising to meet his aggression with her own, she would watch him and how he reacted and as she did this she would be calm. They never argued, they were in new territory and each word said in anger now was another tear in their marriage.

Last night, she had wanted his support and she had wanted him to throw his arms around her. Now he was offering to work on it and she was determined they should end it. The only difference between then and now were the words, 'Laurence, can we talk'.

He insisted on talking it through more and he put away his anger as he took out his reasonableness and vulnerability. They would talk this through more and she was unhappy and uneasy because nothing had been resolved. The weight of her illness fell heavily onto her and she thought she could feel it in her head at the base of her brain, not far from the back of her throat.

They were tired; they went to bed.

Chapter 41

All being said and done, Max was doing very well out of being expelled. He had the newest PlayStation, the newest *Star Wars* game – the one where he could customise his own lightsabre – and he didn't have to go to school.

He was being taken out to restaurants and shops by his mother because she didn't go into work, and his father drove him round to see friends and play football. His mother had told him she would be working less.

Everyone, including his sister, kept asking him if he was okay. Two days after he was expelled his aunt Chloe came to visit. It was just the three of them and after a while he left them to talk in the kitchen. He went to play *Star Wars*, but left the door open so he could half listen to them while he played but at a certain point he noticed their voices missing.

He looked down the corridor and saw that they'd closed the door to the kitchen. He was curious because adults only did this when they were talking about something he wasn't supposed to hear. So, placing his feet on the floorboards that didn't creak, he tiptoed to the door.

'So, the day after you got your results from Sara, you came back and you were both just in the sitting room, staring up at the ceiling?'

'We didn't talk to each other.'

'That's not normal. And he still wants to work this through?'

'We argued last night. He called me cruel and calculating. I have to admit it might have come across as sudden from his perspective but I don't have time to—'

He couldn't tell who was speaking: his aunt sounded surprisingly identical to his mother when their voices were low and behind the kitchen door. Their voices dipped lower and he imagined them mouthing things without any sound because whatever they were talking about must have been that secret. He put his ear right up against the door.

'... going one way when I was healthy. I just want to ask: am I absolutely mad in not telling him? I feel bad that I'm not telling him, of course I do, but for fuck's sake, it's my life, for as long as—'

'Then why don't you tell him? He has to respect your decision.'

'What? And say if I've only got six... even though you think I need you? It's a heck of a lot of rejection for anyone to take... She saw... leaving the house.'

'La-Ree's ego! But you have every right to approach this the way you want to.'

It didn't make sense. He tried to fill in the gaps any which way, but he couldn't think of the words that fitted with what he'd heard. He needed to hear more to make a better guess.

Then a moment later, he was shock-jumped by the doorbell ringing and he ran back into the TV room, spring-stepping on his toes not to make any noise on the floorboards under the carpet.

It was Sara with her daughter and a babysitter for them both.

Chapter 42

Lisa felt fine, but they weren't going to let the sick one drive. Chloe took the keys out of her sister's handbag and gave them to Sara. 'I never took my test,' she explained.

Chloe and Sara climbed in the front, leaving their charge to get in the back. She was grateful to be on her own there, to have a little space to think. She listened to her sister and her closest friend, relative acquaintances talking like old friends, both being more open than she knew them to be, sharing without boundaries around the common ground: Lisa herself. She learned a little bit more of both in the way they spoke to each other.

And as she listened, she realised something – they weren't talking *like* old friends but *as* old friends. Their relationship being another thread to the fabric of Lisa's own life.

They got to Alice's school and she was standing there at the gate as planned. Sara tapped the horn and Alice waved, looked both ways and crossed the road. Lisa felt a rush of protectiveness over her daughter. That morning, Alice had come down and left for school before everyone else, the remnants of her breakfast left on the table.

'Did they give you a hard time skipping class?' asked Sara.

'Nope, all good,' said Alice, climbing into the back with her mother.

'I think if you mention *hospital* and *test results* most schools are going to let a pupil out. Especially if you add *mother* to that,' said Chloe, reminding everyone why they were there and changing the atmosphere in the car. Chloe turned round to her niece. 'How are you holding up?'

*

Since Lisa had told her of her illness, Alice had felt guilty for the blame she'd left at her mother's feet. A memory rose into her head: six months earlier she'd found her mother on the sofa, a book on her lap not being read, staring into space. Alice had walked in and her mother didn't look up and at first she'd thought it was funny and she counted the seconds until her mother noticed her. Her mother said nothing and her lack of acknowledgement gradually stopped being a joke and became something more concerning.

'Hi, Mum,' she'd said, and Lisa had snapped out of wherever she'd been and Alice unfolded a blanket and put it over her mother.

'What's up?' she'd asked, and her mother had said, 'Nothing, darling.'

But it was a *nothing* in which a whole life was living and instead they spoke about the smaller things going on and before long, Alice was late to meet up with friends. But she didn't get up and say she had to leave. Instead, she slipped her phone out by the arm of the sofa chair so that her mother couldn't see her texting her friends to say she didn't feel like heading out. Alice found out later that that had been the day Lisa had had her big argument with Chloe.

She wondered why this memory came to her now, why her subconscious provided it to her in the car with her mother on the way to the hospital.

*

Lisa watched Alice breathe in Chloe's question: 'How are you holding up?' It was all she was thinking about on the way to the hospital: how Alice was holding up in the presence of her mother, godmother and aunt. She worried that perhaps the situation was too much.

'It's a lot to take in,' said Alice, in little more than a whisper.

'Alice knows about Laurence too,' said Lisa. 'That I'm going to leave him.'

'How did it go last night, with Dad?' she asked so that only her mother could hear.

'He wants to work through things. Who knows – maybe we can.' She reached out and held her daughter's hand as the car drove off.

'I don't think you should bother,' said Alice.

A sense of pride filled Lisa. Her daughter was out of place among them with so much less life experience, but she was catching up fast and here she was, brave or scared. Lisa tried to think of something to say to her daughter and she squeezed her hand when she couldn't. It was too much, taking her to the hospital, but as if reading her mind, Alice said, 'I'm glad I'm here.'

There were no cracks in the universe. She looked down, and the rug had still been pulled from under her feet, but instead of nothing it was filled with the moment she was in and the people with her in the car and everything made sense and had purpose.

'Okay,' said Sara, turning round to the mother and daughter in the back of the car and putting the handbrake on, 'we're here.'

The journey had taken no time at all.

Chapter 43

Calm and chaos crowded round Lisa. Here she was, in this waiting room, in this hospital, in this town, in this country, on this planet, in this galaxy, in this universe, living her life, learning how it might end.

But she was not alone. Alice, Sara and Chloe: the women with her were her allies, united to fight for her into any battle; more powerful than a supernova destroying stars; more massive than the Big Bang, created in a moment, a universe of atoms all passing through her now. What was she made of? Atoms of stardust.

What was she made of? Not bones and organs, not her body, not that bit of her that nurtured a tumour. What was her essence once she was gone and what memory of her would be left behind? The imprint of courage and fear.

They were called through to Dr Okoye's office, a small room with only two seats for a patient and their companion. He assured them it was fine if Lisa wanted all of them in the consulting room, that they could crowd in and no one had to wait outside. The doctor and Chloe went out to grab two chairs and by the time they came back, Chloe had discovered several mutual interests and was nattering away as if they were anywhere in the world other than at an oncology appointment. The power of the Chloe Show was limitless and Lisa's sister was here for her. Her sister, who was a living history of Lisa's own self.

She turned around and there was Sara, a doctor who knew what was about to happen, and a friend who had been at her side for more than half her life. A doctor who dealt with life and death, sickness and health and had given her working life to other people. A friend who was ready to drop everything for her.

And next to Lisa was her daughter, with all the worries every teenager went through and more. Friends, fallings-out, break-ups, exams and a family that might not be working as she wanted it to; a child, adolescent and woman all at the same time. She was here for her mother too.

What was Lisa made of? The women by her side.

Before the meeting began, she put up her hand up. She waited there for a moment, hand in the air, then spoke. 'Thank you for all your work, Dr Okoye. Before you say anything: you know Sara; this is my sister, Chloe; and this is my daughter, Alice.' He nodded and shook each of their hands in turn.

'I wanted to say this, before you give me the results, given where we're at and who's here. I wanted to say that I know – or at least it's my expectation – that your diagnosis won't be dissimilar to Dr Stevens'. I suspect that I only have months to live, if I'm lucky, a little over six. Time is all that really matters to me. For some reason I've been saying six, as if that's the magic number.'

Alice sat quietly next to her, with her hand resting on her mother's lap. What Lisa wanted to say was that they weren't here for hope, to watch it burst through at their hour of need and find out that everything was alright, that there was a magical medicine that would cure her. They were here for a diagnosis, a second opinion that would likely be more accurate, but also more of the same.

'Your expectation is fair,' began Dr Okoye going into more detail, but Lisa didn't listen to him, or couldn't, because she had spent so much energy getting herself to the appointment. She half-heard bits of what he said among technical breakdowns and medical walk-throughs. Some of the tumour might be removable, but it was a big operation for small return. Some chemotherapies might work, given the type of cancer, but they were likely only to prolong her life, not put the cancer into remission. What was she made of? Time. Six months of it.

All his technical points – which were really just answers to the question 'How ill am I?' – coalesced around a conclusion, a number which was also just a best guess.

'I think you're right. If we can quickly identify the right chemotherapy, we could be looking at six months. Without it, it's very hard to say a number at all.'

Sara and Chloe had a hand each on her shoulder and back, while she and Alice held hands. All four of them, connected through her own body. What was she made of? The connections that made her whole.

Lisa glanced at Alice, then back to her doctor. He continued. 'But I also wanted to talk to you about something else.' He picked up a small folder and handed it over to Lisa. 'This is an application to join a promising immunotherapy drug trial. It's full but I'm hopeful they can make space for one more patient.'

Chapter 44

Throw a rock into a river, the river keeps flowing. It flows around and over the rock so that there's no noticing the rock is even there. Time keeps flowing and nothing changes. The world keeps turning and three times a day human beings eat a meal.

'How are you feeling?' said Sara to all of them in the car like roll-call on the bus.

'I'm starving,' said Lisa. 'Absolutely starving.'

'Me too,' said Alice.

'Gastropub?' said Chloe. 'I know a good one. A reassuringly expensive one.'

'Would you like to keep it a family thing?' asked Sara.

'Nonsense,' said Lisa. 'There's the family you're given and the family you curate. You *are* family.'

'Mum?' Alice said, leaning in for a hug. 'I'm sorry I've been so horrible to you these last few weeks. I can't come for lunch though. I need to get back to school.'

Chapter 45

When Alice's boyfriend broke up with her, she'd asked him why. She clawed at his reasons, seeing everything he said as he presented them to her, agreeing with him as if agreeing with these things might mean he'd be willing to work them out. In those moments, she was beholden to his explanation. After the break-up, he'd chastised her when she wasn't willing to be friendly, but now she saw it differently.

Sara, Lisa and Chloe dropped her off at the school gates but Alice didn't go back to school. Once their car turned the corner, she walked to the bus stop.

Some lessons stung like bees, quick and learned in an instant; some took time. Youth burned in the cheeks as naivety for anyone see and for anyone to take advantage. By spinning a yarn and telling a lie, an adult could teach a valuable lesson to a teenager, but that lesson takes time.

On the bus Alice texted her father to meet her at home urgently.

One parent could treat her like an adult and tell her they had cancer. The other could treat her like a child and tell her a lie – that her mother wanted an open marriage. When she'd come home early after skipping class on a Friday afternoon and seen a strange woman with her father at the front door, he'd lied to her knowing that her naivety was on offer. Knowing that through her love, naivety would give way to gullibility.

Alice had assumed that her mother didn't mind her father having an affair. It had been possible that her mother had stopped loving him, and she'd guessed that maybe she was having an affair of her own. These were all blanks that Alice had filled in after she'd seen her father that day. Assumptions that over the last two weeks had frightened her, caused her to blame her mother. But first they were lies her father had insinuated so that Alice wouldn't tell her mother what she'd seen. Lies that followed a truth – her mother could be distant.

She wouldn't have called it fear when she found out he was having an affair because she was too immersed in the fear to realise it. But it was fear she felt at the prospect of her parents separating. Fear found its target and became anger. For weeks, her father had sat there, at the kitchen table, on the sofa, in his office, in the car, and allowed her to blame her mother, based on clever, calculated lies that mimicked a truth – her mother could be cold.

Her mother could be sharp and harsh and Alice's sympathy for her father had grown as she thought she witnessed him trying to fix their marriage.

She wasn't going to forgive him. She'd made up her mind that this was unforgivable and it shouldn't have been her responsibility to tell her mother about the affair: it was his. But when her mother had asked for a separation, he'd wanted to work out the problems in their marriage.

By the time Alice turned up at home straight from the hospital, her father was already there. She knew he was scared of her because he had come without asking why he should leave work in the middle of the day. She was going to confront him when she should have been having lunch with her mother after her oncology appointment.

She was already a step beyond hard eyes, fires burning in them so bright, she was blind with anger. A new spectrum of light which was a spectrum of emotion, everything now seen in waves of emotion. How the bus journey home made her angry; how the door to the house stood in her way. She did not want to open it with a key but break it down with a kick. It was a dangerous level of emotion where anything starts to be possible.

Inside, she would find the source, the centre of this universe of anger and the origin of deceit. A star burning on deceit and lies, but at least now she was free of his gravitational pull.

At the door, she tried to imagine how it would unfold, how he would squirm and how he would try and turn it around or how he might come clean. But he wasn't going to manipulate her anymore.

'No!' she took his phone off him, lifted it as high as she could and threw it on the kitchen floor, smashing it to pieces. Max, Sara's daughter and the babysitter were in the other room but she didn't care. 'You don't get to be there for her. She doesn't want you to be. You had an affair. You fucking lied to me. You could have worked on it, you could have been a friend or something but you stopped trying, and you found someone else. You don't get to be there for her now. That's your fucking punishment.'

When Alice left, she left the house as a crime scene that would always carry an imprint of the anger she felt at her father that day. As if walking into the kitchen from that moment on she could say, 'This is where it happened.' She hadn't meant to tell her father about her mother's cancer – Lisa had asked her not to mention it until she'd spoken to Laurence herself.

But Alice had wanted to hurt her father, and it was such low-hanging fruit.

Chapter 46

When the text came through from Alice late that afternoon it was a pleasant surprise: *Can I come see you at work? Would that be okay? Don't worry about school, it's a free period.*

Lisa smiled at the distraction, thought of how brave her daughter had been at the hospital. She replied: *Yes. You should have taken the rest of the day off.*

Then she realised she should have as well. She went back to drafting her proposal to the executive committee. She had been combing her employment contract forensically and calling in on other committee members.

She had decided that the best course of action was to get a deal out of Adam. She'd finished the proposal when a call on her landline came in from Security saying they had 'Someone who is claiming to be your daughter'. Lisa grinned.

'Thank you, Teddy. It pays to be suspicious these days.'

'It does, Lisa. I'm glad you see things my way.'

'Just doing your job, aren't you?

'Exactly.'

'Does she look like me?'

'She does, but then again, that's how they'd get you.'

'Was she polite?'

'Oh, very!'

'Well, in that case, send her up to the fourth floor. But if you don't hear from me, send backup, Teddy.'

Three minutes later, her daughter walked in. 'Hi, Mum. When was I last here?'

'A few years ago at least.'

'Your security guard is a character.'

'Yes, Teddy's very funny. Have a seat,' said Lisa and it was strange to say *have a seat* to her daughter because it really meant *this is my world*. And the world that she was showing her was the world in which she had carved not just a career, but the success most people strived for. A world of achievement far from family life and for the first time ever, she was showing this example to her daughter as an adult.

'How are you feeling?'

'Still fine. I only saw you a few hours ago... Shall we go up to the top floor and have a look at the view?'

They took the lift and Lisa watched Alice take in a little more of her world as she navigated her colleagues' curiosity with politeness until they got to the top floor, to Pam's desk.

'Hello, Pam. You remember my daughter, Alice?'

'Oh, gosh. Yes of course I do,' Pam's eyes bulged at Alice. 'My gosh, you've grown so quickly.' She gave Alice a big, pleasing smile. 'Here,' she said offering Alice a selection of doughnuts.

'Is the boardroom free?'

'Yes, free for the next hour,' said Pam.

Lisa opened the door for Alice and closed it behind them.

'You're having half of this doughnut.'

'No thanks.'

'Your body needs the energy to fight the cancer.'

'Don't use my cancer to wriggle out of Pam's carbohydrates. She'll be heartbroken if you throw it in the bin.'

They sat down and Alice took a bite of the doughnut. 'What's up?' said Lisa. 'Apart from the obvious.'

Alice told her mother everything.

Chapter 47

Lisa called Laurence and while it rang, she imagined the scene between Alice and Laurence; the site of their confrontation. She tried to imagine the ice Laurence had been skating on these last weeks, since Alice had seen him with another woman at their front door. Lisa was shocked at Laurence blaming her for the affair. Shocked, too, that Alice had believed him.

If there were no treatments which could help her fight the cancer, would she have the time to divorce him? Was it worth divorcing him? He would automatically get her assets if they were still married, so what she left to the children would channel through him. She needed to write a new will. She sent a text:

> *I'm surprised you didn't pick up. Please could you take enough of your things for a week or so and find somewhere else to stay. I need time, then we'll speak. For what it's worth, I am sorry you found out that way. L*

She thought for a moment, then added: *We've come to the end of our time.*

Chapter 48

Adam grimaced when he saw her in the doorway to his office. 'I come with an olive branch,' said Lisa.

'Come in,' he said, remaining seated.

She closed the door behind her, handed him a copy of her printed-out deal and sat down on the opposite side of his desk. She watched him read it, watched his pupils dart back and forth over each line, then straight back to the top as he reread it.

There was a knock on the glass door. They both looked round and saw Pam. 'Not now, Pam!' he shouted loud enough for people on the other side of the glass partition to turn their heads.

'Stressed?' asked Lisa.

He scowled at her, then went back to the document. When he got to the bottom a second time, he looked up at Lisa and said, 'These are just bullet points. What's the substance?'

'Only what's written down there.' She saw that it confused him – someone so self-serving couldn't take such an offer at face value: the generosity – or leniency – in it would be treated with suspicion. There was no revenge in her offer, and he couldn't understand that.

'Why?' he asked.

'I think I'm too associated with Jack to be in a senior leadership position under you. I could be CEO, but I've got two children, one of them still young. I'll oversee the transfer of my clients and in an advisory role – maybe Chairman – I can still work for the firm, but on a limited basis. In exchange for my clients, you fold my bonus – which will be guaranteed – into my salary and double it, for one more year. Then I'll leave.'

'I'll want a non-compete for four years. They'll demand it.'

'Then I need some form of remuneration for those four years when I can't work.'

'Fine. We'll give you a lump sum to be negotiated in lieu of the non-compete.'

'Can you wrap it into the salary?'

He frowned. 'Why?'

'I don't want a lump sum coming into my account all at once, that's all.'

He shrugged. 'If payroll don't have an issue, neither do I.'

She put her hand out and he gave back the document. 'So, we're done here, Adam? We have a deal?'

'I'm confused. You got the exec committee together to challenge my position, and now you're going to back me? I'm not playing ball, sorry. No, we don't have a deal until I understand why you're doing this.'

Lisa was torn. She didn't need to tell him. Probably she shouldn't. But then there was humanity, common decency, so that there was no conflict between them anymore.

'I have cancer. Rolling everything into salary increases my life insurance payout.'

Adam lifted up his hands and showed his palms in surrender. 'You don't have to explain any more to me. You would have made a good CEO, Lisa. I'll honour the deal. You have my word.'

And he did.

Chapter 49

'Adam, can I ask you one last thing?' He nodded. 'At the board meeting I missed, did Jack mention me?'

'Lisa, I don't want to get between you two.'

'I can check the meeting minutes, if I have to. But you can save me the bother. Did my position come up at all?'

'You really should speak to Jack on this one.'

'Okay.' She hesitated, slightly confused as she worked out a truth that had been sitting right in front of her. 'Thank you. I think you've just told me what I needed to know anyway.'

She left his office and in a gentle daze made her way back to her own. Eight years ago, when she was leaving for maternity leave, Adam had been handed her clients, by Jack, and they weren't handed back when she returned to work. She was now seeing the wood for the trees.

She sat down and called Jack on her mobile phone.

'How did it go yesterday?' he asked, and as if remembering, 'And how are you?' Lisa was quiet on the line long enough for him to ask, 'Lisa? Are you there?'

'Jack, let me paint you a picture. I was your right-hand woman throughout most of your career. But for some reason, somewhere along the line, you decided to hedge your bets with Adam. You weren't just trying to keep him and the other executives in place. You promised him he'd get your position too and took him on as a mentee. You played Adam and me off against each other, to keep your position as CEO.' It was his turn to keep quiet down the line. 'Only one problem – Adam betrayed you first. How does that theory sound to you? Accurate?'

'I've been trying to keep the ship steady—'

'I can always check the committee minutes. Tell me the truth.'

'Fine,' he said. 'You were the best at business, he was better at internal politics and management. I think he was jealous of you. So, yes, I was succession planning for either one of you, depending on what the business needed.'

'Don't bullshit me anymore, Jack. You held us both off to stay on as CEO. I don't blame you. Divorces are expensive.'

'Lisa, please. Can we meet for a coffee?'

'Goodbye, Jack. Nice knowing you.' She hung up.

Chapter 50

Lisa drove fast with two hands on the wheel but head tilted up slightly to speak into the microphone of the Bluetooth handsfree. She was speeding down the A-road that took her home.

There was that odd moment of quiet, when she heard two sets of background noise: the cars' wheels on the tarmac that came up through the car frame; and the noise from wherever her sister was. 'Where do I stand, then?' Lisa asked.

'As your spouse, Laurence will get everything you have, it's statutory law, unless you have a will that says otherwise, but I'd be astonished if your will does, because you've been married to him and you'd know about it.'

'How quickly can I divorce him?'

'There are two parts of a divorce: the actual divorce; and the financial settlement. The first is admin and should be easy if he's willing to be responsive. The second is a negotiation, can be expensive and take time and money, especially in acrimonious disputes.'

'I don't think he'll fight.'

'Neither do I. Larry's not a twat, just a cheating idiot. But if he chooses to negotiate at the last minute, you have no way of knowing what the outcome will be if you die before it's signed. Money can make people do strange things, and it might be in his interest to delay. You earn a lot more than him but the baseline of divorce is that he would get half of everything you have as a couple.'

'But he's been cheating on me. Doesn't that mean I can take him to the cleaners?'

'That's irrelevant as far as the law is concerned.'

'Really?'

'Yes, stop getting your legal advice from Hollywood.'

'Now I have a rough idea of what my life insurance payout will be, I need to redraft my will so that you and Sara are set up as trustees.'

'Yes, lots to discuss. But we don't have to do that this afternoon.'

Lisa kept her foot to the pedal. She was eager to get home back to Max and Alice, eager to leave the office behind for one of the last times, eager to leave Laurence and have her space and time as she would have it.

'Chloe, what are you doing tonight? Want to have dinner with me and the kids?'

'I'm afraid I've got a date. Next time, for sure.'

'Who with?'

'Love you, bye.'

'With whom?'

Her sister hung up. She smiled thinking of Chloe on a date, it was such a normal thing to do.

Chapter 51

'I'd like to speak to the manager, please.'

Before Lisa got home, she received a text from Laurence saying he had a bag of his things and as requested, had moved out of the house. She wondered where he'd go. She knew he thought hotels were depressing and he was generally too tight-fisted, but he might use their joint account. She wasn't sure many people let their places out on Airbnb in their neighbourhood. So, a friend's? Or even: *hers*?

In his text he had used the words, *temporarily moved out, until we speak*.

She hugged her children when she got in, wondering what to make of the rest of the afternoon with them and what Laurence had said to Max and what he had left for her to say so that she became the voice of their separation. In her mind's eye, they would walk Sebastian while it was still light, then choose a movie at home or go to the cinema. There was no way she was going to cook tonight, so a takeaway seemed likely.

But the universe had other ideas. When she got upstairs, she took off her skirt and left it on the bed. She got into tracksuit bottoms and glanced around the room. Something didn't feel right, the bed that her husband had once used with someone else. She looked further into her evening and saw herself climbing into it alone for the first time.

It wasn't going to happen. So, an hour later she was in the department store, with Max wandering off to find the electronics aisle and Alice at her side. The tired-looking shop assistant sighed. 'I don't see why you want to speak to the manager. She's not going to deliver your new bed.'

'Please, I would be very grateful,' Lisa said.

Very slowly the shop assistant walked off to find the manager.

'Mum, I can't believe you're doing this. Is this what you're like in the office?' asked Alice.

'Let's see what the manager says.'

Later, the assistant came back with the manager who had clearly been briefed on a demanding client. The assistant had her arms folded, standing behind the manager. 'I'm sorry, madam,' the manager began, 'we can't make any exceptions on delivery.'

'But I've bought the most expensive mattress.'

The manager shrugged and shook her head. Catching her daughter slightly off-guard, Lisa said, 'Alice, could you explain why it's so important to have the mattress delivered tonight?'

Her daughter jumped into the role immediately. 'We caught my father cheating in their bed and I don't think my mum wants to spend another night in it.' Both mother and daughter saw the slightest curl in the corner of the manager's smile. She was cracking.

'And the reason why time is important is this,' Lisa took out her test results from earlier in the day.

Alice continued, 'My mum has cancer.' Lisa shrugged because it wasn't a ruse – it was a fact.

The manager considered their double-act, and Lisa wondered if she thought it was a hoax. 'Okay,' said the manager and the assistant unfolded her arms. 'We do have a couple of lorries at the store which technically don't do customer deliveries. I'll see if they've got the time to drop your bed off.'

Ten minutes later, she came back, assistant still in tow. 'How's first thing tomorrow?'

'Oh, that's perfect.'

'You'll be on the couch tonight,' said the manager, 'but better that than a four-week wait. We don't keep the more expensive ones in the store, you see. Also, we won't be able to take your old mattress so you'll have to arrange a collection with the council. Or better yet, get your ex to take it.'

'Thank you so much,' said Alice.

'And you can give your ex-husband a slap from me. Then tell him he's an idiot.'

'Thank you.'

'And good luck with the chemo,' said the manager. 'My brother's in hospital with leukaemia.'

The manager left before Lisa could do anything more than wish her brother good luck. She turned to her daughter. 'Let's go and find your brother.'

'I'll take the couch, Mum. You can have my bed tonight.'

'Would you like the new mattress after I'm gone? If it's not weird, I mean.'

'*If*, Mum. *If!* Dr Okoye's treatment, remember?'

Chapter 52

Once you accept the thing that unsettles you most in the world, everything will be settled.

It was now two weeks since Lisa's diagnosis. Max was asleep upstairs and looking forward to his birthday, but apprehensive about starting a new school. Alice was out but had texted that she would be back soon. Lisa was under a blanket on the sofa, but this evening she was distracted, and even though she had a book open on her lap, she found herself thinking about her son and the anger that might descend on him one day if he were to lose a mother, not to mention when he found out why she'd left his father. The bullying and expulsion would act like kerosene – what an entrance into adolescence.

The familiar clink-clang of the front door sounded down the corridor and into the sitting room, then Alice appeared and to her mother she looked beautiful, with cheeks a little flushed from the cold outside. She swayed the smallest amount as she walked in and said hello with a big smile, standing in the middle of the room. 'Would you like a cup of tea, Mum?'

She came back into the sitting room, concentrating but still spilling tea on the carpet.

'We have to decide if your father can come to Max's birthday,' said Lisa.

Alice placed her tea on the floor near her chair and flopped into it. 'He can call.'

'Max will be upset if he's not there and I'm worried about him,' said Lisa. 'So much of his world is turning upside down.'

'In the same way mine turned, because of Dad?' Alice asked.

'No darling, far more, because when Max sees all this as a young adult, he might not have me around. I know I shouldn't think about that, but I do. Alice, I want to say something, which I know will be difficult to hear, but you need to forgive your father.'

'Never!' Alice was blowing on her tea as she said it with a jolt, spilling more on the carpet.

'And what? You'll live your life without any parents? I'm asking you to prepare to forgive him because he is mostly a good father and he will always have a role in your life.'

'He humiliated me, Mum! But I'm mostly angry because he lost his right to be here, supporting you when he should be.'

'Putting Max first, you won't be able to support him on your own. You've got a flawed man as a father, but there's no breaking news there.'

They sat there sipping tea. Alice put her mug down and chose one of the blankets on the back of the sofa.

'How are you coping?' asked Lisa.

'It's weird not having Dad knocking around the house and I'm still angry with him, for sure, but mostly, Mum, I worry about how you are and if the drug trial will be available.'

Chapter 53

Chloe thought it would be so typical of her sister not to say anything, not because of any meanness or any lofty notions of privacy but because it wouldn't occur to her. She decided to wait until Sara joined them before asking about the drugs trial.

For now, they settled on a bench in the park after their jog, which had become a walk after not much more than a kilometre once Chloe refused to run any further. It was a beautiful late-spring day, almost summer, and the leaves were just coming out on the trees. Her sister's dog was with them too.

'I never understood why you chose such an ugly dog. I'd always assumed it was for the children.'

'Sebastian? No, he's my dog, my companion. Always loyal,' said Lisa.

'It's the shit-picking that puts me off getting a dog.'

'You get used to it. Or maybe you stop thinking about it. Good boy. Shall I get a coffee?'

She watched Lisa walk to the kiosk in the park, order two coffees and come back to the bench, handing her an americano with some milk. While Lisa chatted about the weather and that she hoped that her last summer would be a hot one, Chloe was getting nervous because she wanted to ask about Larry, but she didn't want to upset her sister before Sara joined them.

'*If* it's your last summer, you mean. *If*.'

'Can everyone stop telling me *if* this and *if* that. It's annoying having to deal with a tumour in the middle of my life without everyone saying I'm not dealing with it in the right fucking way.'

Chloe smiled because irritating her sister always made her playful. She pounced. 'Can I ask? Have you spoken to Larry yet?'

Lisa tilted her head forward in suspicion. 'Why? What's Alice been telling you?'

'Just that you still haven't seen or spoken to him since he left the house. I'm not one to jump on his bandwagon, as you know, but he is the father of your children.'

'Well, haven't you done a one-eighty.'

'I'm just saying, if Alice can forgive him after he lied to her...'

'Oh, Christ! We've spoken. I've forgiven him. I forgave him the moment I found out. Sebastian!' Lisa whistled and the dog – which looked more like a black ferret than a dog – ran back to her. She put a lead on him and looped it through the arm of the bench. 'I just don't want to see him right now. I don't have the capacity to deal with his emotions. The thought of him asking me about my cancer makes me shiver. Alice said he's started seeing *the other woman*, of course, which makes me wonder why he was ever interested in working on our marriage.'

'He's probably lonely and this poor woman is the closest person he has, so it makes sense to him to give it a go. It's good though – if he has someone else it might speed up the divorce proceedings.'

'I want it on record,' said Lisa, 'that the most irritating thing about you, Chloe, is your need to play devil's advocate.

But the second-most irritating thing is that when you do, you're occasionally right.'

Lisa's phone rang and she answered, giving a description of where they were in the park. 'Sara's here,' she explained when she hung up.

Chloe spotted her, waving to them from a distance. When Sara got to the bench, she said, 'I suppose I might as well tell you now, rather than waiting for the call this afternoon. I spoke to Dr Okoye about the immunotherapy treatment. The bad news is that your tumour is too developed for them to accept you onto the trial, but the good news is, they aren't going to deny you the treatment either because the medicine is so effective. You'll just be an off-trial patient, assuming you'll agree to it?'

'That's amazing news,' said Chloe, relief flooding and love consuming. She thought of Lisa holding the folder Dr Okoye had handed over in the consulting room, unsure how to interact with the physical manifestation of hope. Her sister could be so despairing.

She looked at Lisa and watched tears form and her go from accepting death to accepting she might have a chance of more life. It would still be touch and go even with the treatment; apparently the first neurologist had said she was already a miracle of science that further symptoms hadn't already arisen.

'That shows how close it is,' said Lisa. 'They don't want someone so ill it will skew the results. When does the immunotherapy treatment start?'

'Tomorrow,' said Sara. 'He has the medicine on site already, delivered from an Oxford University lab last night. Or I could call and maybe we could see him today?'

Chloe wanted to ask Lisa what was going on in her head, but then she saw a smile rounding the corners of her sister's mouth.

Lisa said, ‘I thought there were cracks in the universe. I thought that there was nothing below my feet and that I would fall. But I have you and I have the children. If the treatment works, just think of all that life ahead of me. Give him a call now. Let’s see if I can start the treatment today.’

Chapter 54

The formality was crushing, like a death knell for their marriage, as Lisa knocked on his new front door and a new world was created between them. Shameful because it was all his doing.

Laurence didn't know what to say, didn't know how to address her, so he just said, 'Hi,' and stood to the side to let her in.

The words *mea culpa* had rung in his heart and mind since he had left the house, the day he'd found out about Lisa's cancer and she'd found out about his affair. They rang again as he opened the door.

His wife walked through to his kitchen and he wondered what this presentation of his new life must look like to her, as she glanced around the room, looking through to the living area where his old shirts were draped over the sofa. She stepped on the footpad that opened the bin and saw the boxes of takeaway. Then she looked up at him and smiled. 'How's things?' she said. She could be so like their daughter, when she wanted to be, his wife of nearly two decades.

'Just trying to make the place home, as much as it's worth doing. I don't think I'll be here long.'

'It's a bit IKEA, isn't it,' she said. 'Are you looking for somewhere else? Are you…' – her smile grew broader

– 'looking to move in with your girlfriend?'

On the one hand, Laurence was relieved that Lisa was teasing him and making him squirm a little. It showed, to some extent, that she was past anger. On the other, she was showing just how far over their relationship she was, and he wasn't sure how that made him feel.

'I might. It's complicated.'

'Don't tell me she's married too!'

'She might be. Please, can we talk about something else? Would you like a coffee?' His wife's playfulness at his expense meant this meeting might not be the confrontation he had more than half expected.

He made them coffee in silence punctuated with offers of milk or sugar, then they sat at the kitchen counter, one on each side. They talked about the children: first Max – on the progress of finding him a different school from the one they'd put him in immediately, for the following academic year; then Alice.

'The lies you told Alice, Laurence, they are unforgivable. That I was having an affair as well? What were you thinking? It will take a long time for her to trust you again.'

'You know – and I'll answer your question, just it will take a moment – I was lonely in the marriage too and it was my mistake, maybe *ours*, not to talk about it sooner, years even. I never considered the idea of leaving the family, or breaking it up. Then along came someone who I fell in love with, and I panicked and kicked everything down the line, any conversations with you, any with her. When Alice saw us together, my instinct was to preserve everything and sort it out later. I'm not saying that was okay, I'm explaining my actions. I'm sorry, and even though we've spoken, I'll know it will take a lifetime to repair things with Alice.'

'But why did you want to stay together when I asked for a divorce?'

'Push came to shove, and I wanted to work on the marriage. I didn't know you were sick, did I?'

'But you didn't want to work on the marriage. You chose someone outside our marriage.'

For a while all they did was sip coffee, Laurence conscious that Lisa was most likely here to talk about divorce. 'What do you want to do about separating?'

'I want to divorce and I'd like to do it as quickly as possible.'

'Okay.' Hearing the words, even though he'd known they were coming, Laurence's heart started beating fast, he felt his skin flushing. 'How quickly?'

'If we're both willing, a divorce can happen relatively quickly these days. But there is the question of a financial settlement too, which can take longer.'

'Splitting our assets?'

'Yes.'

'And how do we do that?'

'By agreement. By talking about it now.'

'Now?' he said, surprised. 'Shouldn't we let lawyers do this?'

'That is specifically what I may not have time for,' said Lisa. 'So let's start with what you want. Tell me.'

'Lisa, I'm not comfortable with this. You tell me what you expect to keep, and we can go from there.'

'I asked you first. You go.'

Lawyers seemed sensible because they were unemotional and objective, not to mention a defence from his wife's commerciality. It was hard to be seen as reasonable in his situation, as she earned several times what he did. Their savings were, truth be told, almost all hers. He had put some money in an ISA and had a tiny pension, but nothing else.

Notions started suggesting themselves: he had worked less because he had pulled his weight with the kids. Part of his career had been sacrificed for hers. He would be entitled to half, he'd already researched that online.

'I want, well – I should say *need* – a degree of financial freedom to set myself up outside the family.'

'What do you regard as *freedom*? Be specific.'

'If you keep the house, I'll need some cash to buy somewhere small or rent, and a contribution as I build up my architectural practice again, which will mean reinvesting my income. We can either agree a sum of money each month, or you could make a commitment to pick up the kids' expenses in perpetuity.'

'I think it's important that you continue to contribute to the children's costs. It's an important link to them. Perhaps, if I give—'

'Hold on, don't say "I give". We're in a marriage, everything is technically fifty-fifty, remember?'

Her jaw tensed, 'Okay. If *we* arrange a capital sum as a down payment for a house, then you'll only have a mortgage to pay and some of the children's costs.'

'How much money are we talking about?'

'You need to go and find some properties while I speak to my financial adviser and tie everything up at work.'

'How's that all going?'

'I've taken on an advisory role and I'm stepping back.'

'Your income is coming down?'

'It's complicated.'

'I'd also like a small lump sum to contribute to my pension.'

'Bloody hell, Laurence! Is it not enough that I'm helping you buy a house and giving you extra cash to set yourself up?'

'I'm not asking what your pay-off at work is, am I? I'm not asking for a valuation on your share-options or the house. We don't live extravagantly, and we have a lot of savings, which admittedly are almost all your savings. But we knew that your job paid more when we got married.

'I'm letting you keep our home while I move out – a house we bought together, for which I also contributed to the mortgage. In total, I'm asking for two relatively small lump sums: one to contribute to my pension; and one to help me get a mortgage; plus, a small monthly contribution as I ramp up my architectural practice and get on my own two feet. In total, I bet that's a heck of a lot less than half the value of our assets, let alone your pay-offs, bonuses and share scheme.'

'I'm not happy about it, but fine. It's agreed then.'

He was apprehensive to ask his next question, but it need to be asked while she was in front of him. 'I have one more question before you go, if I may? It's important.'

'Go ahead.'

'I don't deserve to ask this, but may I come to see you in hospital, or would you rather I not?'

She sighed. 'Before we start talking about bedsides, I've just started a drugs trial. The results from the first trial were positive, but it's touch and go if my cancer isn't too developed. However it pans out, hypothetically, it would mean a lot, seeing you at my bedside. Not just because it will be important for the kids to see us being civil together – which it would be – but because I would want you there.'

'I have no right to say this, but it hurt that you didn't tell me about the cancer. It's all I can think about.'

Lisa shook her head. 'Correct, you don't have the right to say that! Do you remember the way you held my hand at night? What context does sleeping with another woman provide to that gesture?'

'I cared for you, I held your hand. But after the last time we made love, you turned away from me. The mixed messages went both ways.'

He was stifling his emotions and could tell from the pauses as she spoke, so was she. 'Laurence, it's not your fault we drifted apart or that we didn't try to work on things – it's both our faults. But I wasn't going to let you feign everlasting love at my deathbed. I know how lonely I felt in our marriage. So lonely that when I suspected you were having an affair, when I was diagnosed with cancer, I said nothing. I think that was because I was giving you an opportunity to come back to me honestly and not out of guilt. I think I was right and fair to give you that opportunity in the way that I did. And part of me wants know, what if you had.

'So, yes, you can be at my deathbed if it comes to that, but you don't get to tell me that I hurt you. I didn't come here to argue. I came to ask you for a divorce and to agree to a settlement.' Lisa got up to leave. 'The world revolves around the sun and the world spins on its axis. A couple drifts apart, a man cheats on his wife and a woman gets cancer. It's just life, Laurence. Let's do what we can for the children now.'

'What does Max know about your illness?'

'Max knows I'm ill. He knows it's serious but he doesn't know that it's life-threatening.'

'And the new school?'

'It's taking time for him to settle in.'

'And Alice?'

'As far as Alice is concerned, I wouldn't put a parenting foot wrong again for the rest of your life. I've got to go, Laurence.'

Chapter 55

'Max, hurry up! You'll be late for your first day!' Lisa shouted up the stairs, listening for signs of how ready or unready her son was. Normally, she'd hear Max's feet thumping around and hurrying up, but today she heard nothing and today, she felt really sick. There were good days and bad days, but this morning was particularly bad. She swore to herself that she would not let Max notice on his first day at his new school. She was calling him down fifteen minutes early so that she could cook them all bacon and eggs.

'Max?' she shouted again.

'Coming,' came a diminutive answer.

In the kitchen, Alice had taken her father's role of making good, strong coffee with a moka pot every morning. On mornings like this, coffee was helpful.

It was not lost on Lisa that it was six months to the day since Sara had given her the results of the CT scan, and that, more or less, Dr Stevens had given her that amount of time. And yet here she was, alive, even if she felt like death. Days like today were hard, but they were also the days she lived for.

Max came downstairs and slid quietly onto his chair and Alice started bombarding him with questions, which

Lisa could tell she did to distract her brother from his nerves. Even so many months later, Lisa wondered if his expulsion would continue to stalk his education up to secondary school. 'Who's up for bacon?'

If Alice saw something that she could do – a task, a thing to lift or a door to open – she'd lunge at it before her mother could. Often, Lisa would smile and say that it wasn't necessary, but today, she was in so much pain that she said nothing when Alice started frying the eggs and taking the bacon out from the grill. Occasionally, she would see the helplessness in Alice's face when she looked at her mother. Her daughter missed nothing.

'How come you're not in school uniform?' Max asked his sister.

'You know Alice finished school,' said Lisa, with a plate of bacon and eggs on toast in front of her. When Alice sat down, the three of them ate their breakfast. Lisa felt less and less hungry as the treatments continued, but in front of her daughter she ate everything she could, stifling the effort of it, showing off a seemingly healthy appetite.

Alice kept up the questions: What was the school like when he visited it over the summer? Had he met his new teachers? Who did he know that already went to the school? They worked like a tonic, as Max became talkative, focusing on the familiar.

Then her children ate porridge and cereal, while Lisa said that she was fine with coffee, and busied herself with stacking the dishes and washing the frying pan. For a brief moment, when she was standing by the sink washing the dishes, part of her vision went dark, just for a moment, and she leaned against the counter for stability and kept on washing the plate. It passed – it had been her left eye again, playing up. She looked over her shoulder and saw that Alice hadn't noticed anything.

'Okay then,' she said, seeing Max with an empty plate in front of him. 'School time.' Max went upstairs to get his bag.

'Everything okay, Mum?'

'I'm very tired today.'

'I can see. You're moving slowly. Do you want me to drive with the L-plates on?'

'Fat chance. It's okay. I can manage.'

They got up and went to the front door and Max came down, step by step. 'Do you have your swimming kit, darling?'

'Yes, Mum.'

'Show me,' she said. Max's eye grew wide.

'Swimming isn't on Monday,' he said.

'It is at this school. Go on, go get it and we'll wait here. Towel, swimming trunks, goggles and a verruca sock. Be quick. We don't want to be late on your first day.'

When she got home, Chloe's car was waiting outside and her sister got out a moment later. They hugged and went inside. 'Coffee?' asked Chloe.

'Herbal tea for me.'

They talked about Max and Alice, and about Laurence, who had moved out of his temporary apartment and into a house with his new girlfriend.

'You know,' said Chloe, 'I think I prefer Laurence now that he's not married to you. We had a really civil conversation at Max's birthday in August.'

'I remember, I was watching you both.'

After a while, there was a knock on the door and Chloe went to let Sara in. She'd been on holiday and was looking tanned and healthy.

'You heard Alice's news?' asked Chloe.

'Exam results?'

'Top of her year group at school.'

'No,' corrected Lisa, 'top in the county.'

They settled in and talked about old stories, from childhood to university. They laughed and made toast and at 11 a.m., Chloe opened a bottle of wine that was in the fridge.

'How is everything?' she asked when she sat back down with her wine, and Sara looked up from her tea. Chloe knew, as they all did, the results of the immunotherapy, radio and chemo treatments.

Now there's a question, thought Lisa. Today, so far, she'd been sick in the toilet before the children were up. Her bones ached, her head ached and her stomach didn't much like having food in it. She'd almost fainted doing the washing-up. But still, none of that mattered. What mattered was that she'd driven her son to his first day at his new school, then dropped her daughter off at her part-time job, and the month before, she'd been there for Alice's exam results. What mattered was that the tumour had shrunk in size.

'Another day in paradise,' she said wryly.

Epilogue

Dearest Max

I think I am mostly writing this letter to remind myself what I'm fighting for. It is too hard to imagine that you might open this alone. When I first thought to write it, I believed I had only months to live. Now there seems to be a fighting chance at a healthy life.

I have just read you a bedtime story and you are now fast asleep in your bed. In the last few weeks I have found myself coming up to your room and watching you sleep.

One of the purposes of this letter, if the worst comes to the worst, is to console you and compensate you for my loss. Can you imagine that? In exchange for losing your mum while still a child, and in exchange for not having a mum for the rest of your life, you get this and the handful of other letters which I have decided to write throughout my treatment. If I die, it will not be fair, but it is all I can give you beyond the time we have now. I'm sure you will be angry, perhaps so angry that it may become your life's work processing it.

Don't be alone in your anger. I never thought I'd find myself alone, but there I was one morning on the school run outside Sara's clinic, trying to process my diagnosis and telling no one about it. I wasn't alone. I had all the people around me I needed, but I just had to remind myself of this. I have you, I have Alice, and I have Sara and Chloe.

You know me as Mummy. You called me Lisa once as a joke but actually I am both those people. I am also Mum to your sister, a daughter to your grandparents, a sister to your aunt, a sister to Sara, and a friend and colleague to so many more.

I met your dad in my mid-twenties and we had your sister not long after that. We waited eight years to have you so that we could experience more of our young adulthood. We had you in our mid-thirties. While raising your sister, your dad and I built our lives, careers and the place you call home.

It is wonderful to see your sister being protective of you.

You will eventually ask – or find out – why I left your dad. I know how angry you will be and how it might swallow you whole and there's so little I can do to help you. Forgive your dad. Perhaps with more time, or more certainty of time, we might have worked on our marriage, but we came to the natural end of our relationship.

There is no meaning of life, no grand philosophy. A woman gave birth and became a mother a second time and eight years later she developed cancer.

But there is meaning in life and this is what we make for it, in how we live and who we live with. Raising you and your sister and feeling isolated from your dad, I forgot the meaning that my sister and Sara gave me. Their support in these recent months has reminded me that they have been there for me as long as I've known them.

You were expelled from school last spring. It wasn't fair how you were treated, but what you do from this point, however, is on you. Not everyone needs school and university, but I think you might. You will need to figure this out for yourself.

I am going to keep these letters, but they will go to your aunt Chloe if I die. I think of you in the future, of your aunt Chloe giving these letters to you and you both reading them together. I have asked her to present them to you when you are down or in trouble.

I imagine the life you will have in the next ten years. Will you have met your first girlfriend by then, I wonder? Then I imagine the ten years after that, and the ten years after that, and so on. Remember and hold onto the nine or so years we've already had together, if that's all we get. Some do not even get that. Wherever I will be, I am excited to watch your life pan out.

If I die, you might feel the whole world is against you, that it's unfair and cruel. But you are about to become a young adult: the world will be at your feet. So, live your life, and live it well.

With all the love in the world,

Your mum, Lisa.

Firstly, I would like to thank the readers, for whom I wrote this book. Please do recommend it if it moved you.

Getting this book finished required input and support from so many people. I would like to thank my parents, brothers, sisters and friends for reading drafts and giving notes and encouraging me along the way. I would like to thank Joanna, Gale, Heather and Helen, who helped me get the book into a finished product that could be on a shelf.

Lastly, I would like to thank the independent bookshops, and the booksellers within them, not only for helping me to choose my next read, but also creating a sense of community among readers and writers alike – so important in the often lonely pursuit of writing. Their work breathes much life into the literary industry.

A note on the text

The medical conditions in the novel are not necessarily consistent with a specific medical condition. Portrayals were altered for dramatic effect. No medical professionals were consulted on this portrayal.